Daisy Miller

A Dark Comedy of Manners

TWAYNE'S MASTERWORK STUDIES

ROBERT LECKER, GENERAL EDITOR

DAISY MILLER

A DARK COMEDY OF MANNERS

Daniel Mark Fogel

TWAYNE PUBLISHERS • BOSTON

A Division of G. K. Hall & Co.

Daisy Miller: A Dark Comedy of Manners
Daniel Mark Fogel

Twayne's Masterwork Studies No. 35

Copyright 1990 by G. K. Hall & Co.
All rights reserved.
Published by Twayne Publishers
A division of G. K. Hall & Co.
70 Lincoln Street, Boston, Massachusetts 02111

Book production by Gabrielle B. McDonald
Copyediting supervised by Barbara Sutton
Typeset by Compset, Inc., Beverly, Massachusetts

Printed on permanent/durable acid-free paper
and bound in the United States of America

Library of Congress Cataloging in Publication Data

Fogel, Daniel Mark, 1948–
    Daisy Miller : a dark comedy of manners / Daniel Mark Fogel.
        p.   cm. — (Twayne's masterwork studies ; no. 35)
    Bibliography: p.
    Includes index.
    ISBN 0-8057-7975-2 (alk. paper).—ISBN 0-8057-8025-4 (pbk. : alk.
paper)
    1. James, Henry, 1843–1916.   Daisy Miller.   I. Title.
    II. Series.
    PS2116.D33F64   1990
    813'.4—dc20
                                                      89-1527
                                                      CIP

For my grandparents,
Harry and Anna Finkelstein
Harry and Elizabeth Fogel

CONTENTS

NOTE ON THE REFERENCES
AND ACKNOWLEDGMENTS

Parenthetical references to *Daisy Miller* are to the Norton Critical Edition *Tales of Henry James,* edited by Christof Wegelin (New York: W. W. Norton, 1983). I chose this text because it is widely available in paperback and because as a reprint of the first English Edition (Macmillan & Co., 1879) it presents the story in a form very close to its first publication in *Cornhill Magazine* (June and July 1878). There are, in fact, only a few minor changes in wording between the *Cornhill* version of the text and the first English Edition reprinted by Wegelin. On the other hand, there are hundreds of substantive differences between these early versions of *Daisy Miller* and the revision Henry James prepared some thirty years later for the New York Edition of *The Novels and Tales of Henry James.* Since I discuss the revised *Daisy Miller* later in this book, suffice it to say here that the choice of the earlier version is made easy by two considerations: first, it is the version most frequently taught and read; second, it is, according to the consensus of James scholars, the superior version.

Anyone writing about *Daisy Miller* owes a large debt of gratitude to previous commentators on that tale and on Henry James generally, above all to Leon Edel. In my notes I have tried to acknowledge all specific points of indebtedness of which I am aware. I simply wish here to acknowledge the general debt. More particularly, my work on this book has been greatly facilitated by the work of my graduate research assistant, Jon

Daisy Miller

Thompson. I am grateful to Mr. Thompson for his hard work and for the acute intelligence he has brought to it. I am also grateful to the Department of English at Louisiana State University (and to its chairman, John R. May) for having made Mr. Thompson's services available to me. Adeline R. Tintner lent me Timothy Cole's 1882 white-line wood engraving (number 1 of 237) of Henry James, and John Wood photographed it for use as the frontispiece of this book. I am grateful to them both for their generous assistance.

HENRY JAMES
White-line wood engraving (1/237) by Timothy Cole, 1882
Collection of Adeline R. Tintner
Photo by John Wood

CHRONOLOGY:
HENRY JAMES'S LIFE
AND WORKS

1843	Henry James born 15 April at 21 Washington Place, New York City (eighteen months after his oldest sibling, philosopher-to-be William James), to Henry James, Sr., a religious philosopher, and Mary Robertson Walsh. Family lives abroad in England and France from 1843 to 1845.
1847	Family moves to 58 W. 14th St., New York City. Frequent visitors—friends of James's father—include Horace Greeley, William Cullen Bryant, and Ralph Waldo Emerson.
1855	Family departs 17 June for three-year European sojourn in France, England, and Switzerland.
1858	Family returns to America, settling in Newport, Rhode Island. Henry studies art there with the painter John La Farge.
1859	Family returns to Europe. Henry attends engineering school in Geneva and studies German in Bonn.
1861	Outbreak of the Civil War. Suffers, in October, while helping to fight a stable fire, a back injury, the notorious "obscure hurt," which kept him out of the war.
1862	Enters Harvard Law School.
1863	Withdraws from Harvard to devote himself to writing.
1864	Family moves to Boston. First story, "A Tragedy of Error," published (unsigned). Begins writing book reviews for *North American Review*.
1865	First signed tale, "The Story of a Year," published in the *Atlantic Monthly*. Vacations with his beloved cousin Minnie Temple in the White Mountains, where they are joined by Oliver Wendell Holmes, Jr., the future Supreme Court justice.
1866	Begins lifelong friendship with editor and novelist William Dean Howells. Family settles in Cambridge, Massachusetts.

1869	Departs February on first adult solo trip to Europe. In England meets Charles Darwin, George Eliot, John Ruskin, Edward Burne-Jones, and others. Travels to Paris (May), Switzerland (summer), and Italy, where he stays for four months.
1870	Returns to England early in year. Minnie Temple dies ("she *represented* . . . in my life several of the elements or phases of life at large—her own sex . . . but even more *Youth*"). Returns to Cambridge in May. Visits Ralph Waldo Emerson in Concord, Massachusetts, for a few days.
1871	First novel, *Watch and Ward,* serialized in the *Atlantic Monthly.*
1872	Travels with his Aunt Kate and sister Alice on European tour (May–October). Spends fall in Paris, befriending James Russell Lowell. Guides Emerson through the Louvre.
1873	Spends most of year in Italy, chiefly Rome. For the first time, earns enough from writing to support himself.
1874	Returns to America in September.
1875	Lives and writes in New York. First three books published: *A Passionate Pilgrim and Other Tales, Transatlantic Sketches* (travel essays), and *Roderick Hudson* (which he later would call his first novel, ignoring *Watch and Ward*). In November, returns to Paris, where he enjoys the friendship and literary society of Ivan Turgenev, Gustave Flaubert, Émile Zola, Alphonse Daudet, Guy de Maupassant, and others.
1876	Begins decade-long residence at 3 Bolton St., Piccadilly, London.
1877	*The American* (novel) published. Meets Robert Browning.
1878	*Daisy Miller* published in *Cornhill Magazine.* Pirated editions in America are best-sellers. *Daisy* establishes his fame in the United States and England and makes him a celebrity. Meets Alfred Lord Tennyson, George Meredith, and James McNeill Whistler. *The Europeans* (novel) serialized.
1879	*Daisy Miller* published in book form. Meets Robert Louis Stevenson, who becomes a close friend. Publishes first book-length study of an American writer, *Hawthorne.*
1880	*Washington Square* published. Serialization of first masterpiece, *The Portrait of a Lady,* in *Macmillan's Magazine* (England) and *Atlantic Monthly* (United States), begins in October and continues through November 1881.
1881	Revisits America for first time in six years.
1882	Visits the Henry Adamses in Washington. Mother dies in Jan-

	uary. Returns to England in May. Summoned home in December but father dies (18 December) before his arrival.
1883	Returns to London. Macmillan publishes collected novels and tales (14 vols.). Death of brother, Garth Wilkinson.
1884	Befriends John Singer Sargent. Sister Alice, ailing, settles nearby. Publishes "The Art of Fiction."
1885	Serialization of the novels *The Princess Casamassima* (in *Atlantic Monthly*) and *The Bostonians* (in *Century Magazine*); both come out as books in 1886.
1886	Moves to flat at 34 De Vere Gardens West, Kensington, London.
1887	Spends half the year in Italy, writing "The Aspern Papers" and other tales.
1889	Dramatizes *The American.*
1890	*The Tragic Muse* (novel) published. Meets Rudyard Kipling. The novelist and short story writer Constance Fenimore Woolson moves to England to be near James.
1891	Abandons writing novels (but not short stories) in order to pursue popular success as a playwright.
1892	Alice James dies.
1894	Woolson commits suicide in Venice. Travels to Italy to visit her grave and to help settle her affairs.
1895	Booed at opening of his play, *Guy Domville*, abandons theater to return full-time to the art of fiction ("I take up my *own* old pen again—the pen of all my old unforgettable efforts and sacred struggles. . . . It is now indeed that I may do the work of my life").
1896	*The Spoils of Poynton* (novel) serialized in *Atlantic Monthly* (published in book form, 1897).
1897	*What Maisie Knew* (novel) published. Begins friendship with Joseph Conrad. Midway through *Maisie*, begins to dictate to a typist because of writer's cramp; will dictate fiction for the rest of his career. Signs a twenty-one-year lease on Lamb House in Rye, which will become his principal residence.
1898	*The Turn of the Screw* (novella) published, his biggest popular success since *Daisy Miller.*
1899	*The Awkward Age* (novel) published. Purchases Lamb House. Sees brother William for first time in six years. Meets young sculptor Hendrik Christian Anderson. James B. Pinker becomes his literary agent.

1900	Shaves off beard worn since Civil War. Begins *The Ambassadors* (novel).
1901	*The Sacred Fount* (novel) published.
1902	*The Wings of the Dove* (novel) published. Writes "The Beast in the Jungle."
1903	*The Ambassadors* published. Meets Edith Wharton.
1904	*The Golden Bowl* (novel) published. In August, begins year-long tour of the United States after twenty years' absence. Visits Wharton, meets President Theodore Roosevelt, and lectures widely.
1905	Returns to England (July). Begins revisions of novels for the New York Edition of *The Novels and Tales of Henry James* (24 vols., 1907–1909).
1906	Begins writing eighteen prefaces for the New York Edition.
1907	*The American Scene* (travel essays) published. Motors in France with Wharton. Last visit to Italy.
1910	Nervous breakdown. Returns to America with William James (August). Deaths of brothers Robertson and William.
1911	Returns to England. Fearing loneliness at Lamb House, resides at Reform Club in London.
1912	Summers at Lamb House. Sees much of Edith Wharton.
1913	*A Small Boy and Others* (autobiography) published. Moves into London flat at 21 Carlyle Mansions, Cheyne Walk, Chelsea. Some 275 friends and admirers subscribe to seventieth-birthday tribute, including gifts of a Sargent portrait and of a golden bowl. Summers at Lamb House.
1914	*Notes of a Son and Brother* (autobiography) published. Summers at Lamb House. Horrified by the war ("Black and hideous to me is the tragedy that gathers, and I am sick beyond cure to have lived on to see it"). Accepts chairmanship of American Volunteer Motor Ambulance Corps. Visits wounded in hospitals.
1915	Becomes a British citizen. Suffers a stroke on 2 December.
1916	Order of Merit conferred by George V on New Year's Day. Dies 28 February. Funeral in Chelsea Old Church. Ashes buried in family plot in Cambridge Cemetery, Cambridge, Massachusetts.

1

HISTORICAL CONTEXT

Henry James was thirty-five years old in 1878, when the run-away success of *Daisy Miller: A Study* made him a celebrity in both England and America. Known to the world as Henry James, Jr.—he did not drop the "Jr." from his name until 1883, after the death of his father, religious philosopher Henry James—he had applied himself to literary art full-time for some fifteen years, and he was already the author of more than thirty tales, of three novels (*Watch and Ward, Roderick Hudson,* and *The American*), of a book of travel essays, and of numerous essays and reviews on literature and art. Although James made very little money from the American sales of *Daisy Miller* because of his failure to secure an American copyright, editions pirated in New York and Boston sold at a breakneck pace. The edition in Harper's Half-Hour Series sold twenty thousand copies in a few weeks. In London, James was feted as a literary lion. The winter after *Daisy Miller* came out (1878–79), he dined out at least 140 times. He was sought after as a guest not only for his new celebrity but also for his famous acerbic wit and his considerable personal charm. As the novelist Rebecca West

1

wrote in a book-length study of James published the year of his death (1916), "On London staircases everyone turned to look at the American with the long, silky, black beard which, I am told by one who met him then, gave him the appearance of 'an Elizabethan sea captain.'"[1]

Some of the works James wrote before *Daisy Miller* have by now been long established as classics of American literature (notably *The American*), but none of them had had—or have had since—such astonishing success with the public. James wrote the tale, moreover, after a period in which he felt he had been obliged to spend a great deal of time writing journalism (travel sketches, reviews, articles) and fiction designed to please editors more than to satisfy his own ambitions and standards as an artist (works he called "potboilers"). Nevertheless, as his comments in a letter of January 1878 to his brother William indicate, he was poised for literary greatness, primed to make his mark:

> As regards other matters my London life flows evenly along . . . If I keep along here patiently for a certain time I rather think I shall become a (sufficiently) great man. I have got back to work with great zest after my autumnal loafings, and mean to do some this year which will make a mark. I am, as you suppose, weary of writing articles about places, and mere potboilers of all kinds; but shall probably, after the next six months, be able to forswear it altogether, and give myself up seriously to "creative" writing. Then, and not till then, my real career will begin.[2]

Within three months James had written *Daisy Miller* and had received an acceptance for its publication in the *Cornhill Magazine* (edited, incidentally, by Leslie Stephen, who would become, four years later, the father of Virginia Woolf.)

Daisy Miller may be said, then, to mark a watershed in Henry James's artistic development. It was followed in rapid succession by two short novels that are now considered minor masterpieces, *The Europeans* (1878) and *Washington Square*

(1880). And it was clearly preparatory to James's first incontestably great novel, *The Portrait of a Lady* (1881). In vesting innocence and a sense of freedom in an attractive, unmarried American girl in *Daisy Miller,* and then in showing how Daisy comes to grief in conflict with European conventions, James was rehearsing the theme of the much greater novel he would soon write: Isabel Archer, the heroine of *The Portrait of a Lady,* "has dreamed of freedom and nobleness" but "finds herself in reality ground in the very mill of the conventional."[3]

Not only was the publication of *Daisy Miller* a pivotal moment in James's career; it also may be said to be a turning point in the development of American literature. Despite his decision in the last year of his life to become a British citizen, James was an essentially American author, and with the works that he wrote beginning with *Daisy Miller* he conferred on our national literature a stature in the wider world of letters that it had never before enjoyed. At the same time he gave enduring form to some of the foundational myths of modern American literature. He did not invent the international novel—in this genre he had predecessors such as Hawthorne in *The Marble Faun*—but he made it recognizably his own turf. From *Daisy Miller* on, American, English, and European readers looked on Henry James as the master of the novel of international contrasts. Most of his novels and tales involve their protagonists in transatlantic quests for experience: new situations and unprecedented dilemmas—created by the American heroes' and heroines' immersion in European manners, culture, and civilization—lead them to new perceptions so profound that their selves are transformed. In his title character, Daisy Miller, furthermore, James created the paradigm of a central American myth, the myth of the American girl as free, spontaneous, independent, natural, and generous in spirit. Of the greatest of his novels to come, only *The Ambassadors* (1903) does not center on the mythic figure of the American girl, for we see later embodiments of the spirit of Daisy Miller in Isabel Archer in *The Portrait of a Lady,* in

Millie Theale in *The Wings of the Dove* (1902), and in Maggie Verver in *The Golden Bowl* (1904). I might add that of all of the white male authors who have dominated the canon of American literature, Henry James is the outstanding exception to Leslie Fiedler's argument that the classic American writers are inept in portraying women, for, particularly from *Daisy Miller* forward, James's fiction is distinguished by his remarkable empathy with the minds and hearts of his female characters.[4]

In 1879, the year after *Daisy Miller* appeared in the *Cornhill Magazine,* James published what was the first book-length study of an American writer, *Hawthorne.* There he provided an implicit justification of his own decision to live and work overseas. James begins with a quotation from Hawthorne's own preface to *Transformation* (the title under which *The Marble Faun* was published in England): "No author, without a trial," Hawthorne wrote, "can conceive of the difficulty of writing a romance about a country where there is no shadow, no antiquity, no mystery, no picturesque and gloomy wrong, nor anything but a commonplace prosperity, in broad and simple daylight, as is happily the case with my dear native land." James goes on to comment on the "thinness" and "blankness" of "the crude and simple society in which" Hawthorne lived: "It takes so many things, as Hawthorne must have felt later in life, when he had made the acquaintance of the denser, richer, warmer European spectacle—it takes such an accumulation of history and custom, such a complexity of manners and types, to form a fund of suggestion for a novelist."[5] In *Daisy Miller,* with its skillful use of such evocative settings as the Castle of Chillon and the ruins of the Colosseum in Rome, James drew, as we shall see, on the shadow, antiquity, mystery, and gloomy and picturesque wrong of Europe. Even more important, in presenting a realistic social comedy about misunderstandings between the Millers of Schenectady, New York, and the Europeanized Americans of Geneva and Rome, James drew on "a complexity of manners and types" afforded him in rich measure by the European scene but absent, in his view, in democratic America, famous for its leveling of manners.

Even so, James remains an American author, as the conflict between Americans and Europeanized Americans (*not* Europeans) in *Daisy Miller* suggests. Yet James was at the same time the most cosmopolitan of novelists. He came to be fluent in Italian and French, came to be a familiar of the great Continental writers of his age (for example, Turgenev and Flaubert), and, as his philosopher brother remarked after Henry had lived for many years in England, "He's really . . . a native of the James family, and has no other country."[6] Being a male native of the James family meant being raised to value personal freedom above everything else—freedom of conscience, freedom of thought, freedom of feeling.[7] That is why, even though James is an unsparing critic of the follies and limitations of his American girls, his Daisies, Isabels, Maggies, and their sisters, he adores them for their lively assertion of personal independence, which is at once a national trait and a mark of their creator's having been "a native of the James family." As James's father wrote, his aim in his eccentric education of his children was to surround them "as far as possible with an atmosphere of freedom."[8]

Daisy Miller, finally, belongs to the early stage of James's career, a period during which he excelled at realistic social comedy and satire. In the following decade he moved from realism to the naturalism to which he was exposed through his interest in French literature and his acquaintance with such leading French naturalists as Émile Zola. Then, in the late 1890s, he experimented with increasingly psychological novels, works that record the inner drama of consciousness. He was becoming in this experimental phase the founder of radical international modernism, the forerunner of James Joyce and Virginia Woolf. In his last, great novels of 1902–1904, he achieved a dense fusion of realism, naturalism, and poetic symbolism. His prose style became, throughout his career, increasingly complex, marked in its late stages by long sentences with elaborate

syntax, though even before *Daisy Miller* (which is comparatively simple in style) William James told Henry that his "style
ran a little more to *curliness* than suited the average mind."[9] But
despite the many distinct phases through which James developed as an artist, some elements of his work remain constant,
foremost among them the thematic keynote sounded so clearly
in *Daisy Miller*, the keynote, as Ezra Pound put it, of "the major
James, of the hater of tyranny," the champion of "human liberty, personal liberty, the rights of the individual against all sorts
of intangible bondage!"[10] There was passion in James's love of
personal liberty, as Pound observed. In chapter 3, on the critical
reception of the work, we see that passion echoed, sometimes
in odd ways, in the responses readers have had from the first to
Daisy Miller: A Study.

2

THE IMPORTANCE OF THE WORK

Late in life Henry James expressed irritation over the dispro-
portionate attention the public lavished on *Daisy Miller* compared to its interest in the rest of his work.[11] He was
disappointed with the sales of the New York Edition of his
works (1907–9), and he had never enjoyed the regularly best-
selling status of popular contemporary novelists such as Owen
Wister and Mrs. Humphrey Ward or of his friend Edith Wharton; his chagrin that at least some of his other works did not
share the bright limelight of *Daisy Miller* is understandable.
Most James specialists, moreover, and most general readers
would agree that James wrote many much greater, more important works than *Daisy*: the major novels, for instance (*The Portrait of a Lady, The Ambassadors, The Wings of the Dove,* and
The Golden Bowl), and such short stories as "The Pupil," "The
Beast in the Jungle," and "The Jolly Corner." Why, then, has
Daisy Miller outshone these allegedly superior works, at least
in overall sales and number of readers, making it what James
called "the ultimately most prosperous child of my inven-
tion"?[12] Why do we continue to read, study, and teach this

comparatively early novella? Why, in short, does *Daisy Miller* matter?

There are many possible answers to these questions, some of which are implied in the observations about *Daisy Miller* offered in the preceding chapter. *Daisy Miller* is the prototypical "international theme" story, and Daisy herself is the paradigm of the international "American girl." The story thus combines the sharp social observation of literary realism with the power of its embodied myths—and this combination may go some distance toward explaining the attraction of the work for general readers as well as for teachers and students.

But such an explanation of its importance and continuing appeal is only partial and, by itself, quite inadequate. We do not continue to read and enjoy the tale for its historical status as the originating point of certain American myths. We might offer further partial but still inadequate explanations by pointing to the stylistic felicity of the tale, its mixture of satire and poetry, its evocation of the melodramatic pathos of the beautiful, dead girl (a recurrent theme in popular culture, as the famous opening of Erich Segal's shamelessly sentimental *Love Story* demonstrates), and its skillful use of Winterbourne as a conventional, often mistaken, but educable observer (foreshadowing the sophisticated use of such "central intelligence" characters in James's later, more complex fiction). Even its length, on a more pedestrian plane, can be considered a factor—very long for a short story but, compared with the major novels of James and his contemporaries, a shorter, easier, and thus, for many readers, far more palatable "read."

As a reader who finds each return to *Daisy Miller* rewarding and gratifying, I would suggest that, beyond these partial explanations, the major keys—there are certainly more than one—to the continuing success and significance of *Daisy Miller* lie in the still vital and engaging issues that James develops in the tale about the role of convention and stereotyping in the human community, about our vulnerability to self-deception, and about the proper relations between men and women and between parents and children. The specific social taboos that Daisy Miller violates—for example, her unchaperoned excursions with Winterbourne and with Giovanelli—may seem quaintly dated, but it is a mistake to emphasize that the manners portrayed are outmoded, just as it would be to dismiss the great nineteenth-century novels of unhappy marriage (Tolstoy's *Anna Karenina*, Flaubert's *Madame Bovary*, and James's own *The Portrait of a Lady*, among others) because their heroines could have solved their problems had divorce been as easy then as it is now, or to suggest that *Hamlet* is no longer relevant because we are no longer subject to a cultural imperative for personal revenge.

The drama of *Daisy Miller* is in large part the drama of Winterbourne's confusion about Daisy, his continuing, baffled attempts to understand her and to "type" her. The straitlaced American matrons in the tale, Mrs. Costello and Mrs. Walker, simply stereotype Daisy as a disreputable girl. To Winterbourne's credit, he struggles against such stereotyping most of the time, even though he himself is extremely conventional. But when he mistakenly takes Daisy's behavior on the occasion of her midnight excursion to the Colosseum as a confirmation of the matrons' stereotype of her, he succumbs to their way of thinking and becomes the agent of a society that is harmful, even evil, in its determination to type people and to shun those who do not conform rather than to see and to appreciate them in their unique individuality. And yet we also see that Daisy's headstrong failure to heed warnings about nighttime excursions in malarial Rome leads to her death and, more generally, that her utter disregard of convention makes it almost impossible for her to get into effective relation with other people, thus isolating her from the community whose values and norms she ignores.

Thus, in condemning stereotyping yet affirming the value of convention as essential to human relations, James created in

Daisy Miller what Richard A. Hocks has called "a true dialectical inquiry."[13] The same dialectical complexity may be observed in James's handling of the parent-child relation in *Daisy Miller*. On the one hand, we admire Daisy's spirited independence; on the other, we see that James condemns absentminded Mrs. Miller and the physically absent Mr. Miller for their utter failure to discipline their children, to control them, and, ultimately, to protect them, not just from social evils (e.g., Daisy's ostracism) but from the very real physical dangers of the world (the malaria to which Daisy succumbs). The dilemma to which James points here remains pressing today; the failure of parenting—the breakdown of the family and of its role in socializing children and in regulating and normalizing their behavior—is an ongoing crisis in American civilization.

Both of these major themes—the theme of stereotyping and convention and the theme of parental failure—are related to two other major issues, sexual politics and self-deception. Winterbourne places young women in categories: they may be innocent, they may be "great coquettes" (10), or they may be immoral, "light" (40). In any one of these cases his conception of himself as a gentleman would prescribe a certain mode of behavior. His problem with Daisy is that he cannot determine her category and therefore does not know how to conduct himself. As Lauren Cowdery remarks, in part "James's accomplishment is to induce in his readers a revulsion" against this "conventional system" of sexual stereotypes and "to call that system into question."[14] At the same time, Winterbourne's self-knowledge is incomplete; he is unable to acknowledge the extent to which his interest in Daisy is underlain by fantasies in which she is reified as the object of illicit sexual desire. Insofar as he believes she is innocent, the conscious gentleman Winterbourne would be her protector, but in his buried imaginings he brutalizes her as a sexual object. Again, therefore, the issues that James develops in *Daisy Miller* are scarcely outmoded—they are very much with us today.

Finally, as the victim of a system of conventions that she neither appreciates nor understands, Daisy is an embodiment of the free spirit crippled by ignorance and caught in an entrapping world.[15] Henry James understood that life is a struggle, that civilization is at once inestimably valuable, regularly oppressive, and terribly fragile, and that we all must try to live as best we can despite our own vulnerability to self-deception and our own sad capacity for exploitation of others, for cruelty, and for sheer stupidity. *Daisy Miller* remains important because, beyond our enjoyment of James's sharp social observation, of his sparkling comedy, and of his gift for phrasing, our fascination with Daisy and Winterbourne is our fascination with ourselves; their predicaments are ours, and the puzzles of their lives, the puzzles of our own.

3

CRITICAL RECEPTION

After Henry James himself, the first reader of *Daisy Miller: A Study* was John Foster Kirk, the editor of *Lippincott's Magazine* in Philadelphia. We do not know Kirk's reaction to the story, only that he "promptly" rejected it with an absence of comment that James later said he found "grim." A friend (probably Leslie Stephen or William Dean Howells) suggested to James that Kirk might have thought the tale "an outrage on American girlhood." Perhaps, too, James later speculated, Kirk had thought *Daisy Miller* too long; it was a *nouvelle*—a short novel, therefore, not a short story—a "type, foredoomed at the best, in more cases than not, to editorial disfavour."[16] The second reader was Leslie Stephen, who must have liked the tale; he launched it on its remarkable success in the journal he edited, the *Cornhill Magazine*.

We have already noted the huge popularity *Daisy Miller* gained immediately with the reading public. It was long assumed, however, that critical reaction was much less favorable. This assumption seems to have originated with some early comments by or attributed to William Dean Howells. In "The Contributor's Club," a regular column in the *Atlantic Monthly*, which Howells then edited, there appeared a denunciation of "the silly criticisms which have been printed, and the far sillier ones which are uttered in regard to Mr. James's Daisy Miller. . . . It is actually regarded as a species of unpardonable incivism [lack of civic or patriotic feeling] for Mr. James, because he lives in London, to describe an underbred American family traveling in Europe." Thus opined "The Contributor's Club" in March 1879, in the same vein as this comment from the same column the month before: "I am shocked to find that what I gratefully accepted as an exquisitely loyal service to American girlhood abroad is regarded by some critical experts as 'servilely snobbish' and 'brutally unpatriotic.'"[17] These comments, long thought to have been offered by Howells himself, were in fact penned by Constance Fenimore Woolson (February) and by John Hay (March).[18] A few months later Howells himself wrote to James Russell Lowell, "Henry James waked up all the women with his *Daisy Miller*, the intention of which they misconceived, and there has been a vast discussion in which nobody felt very deeply, and everybody talked very loudly. The thing went so far that society almost divided itself into Daisy Millerites and anti-Daisy Millerites."[19]

There was indeed an abundance of contemporary critical comment on *Daisy Miller*, both in its magazine version and in the pirated and authorized book versions of 1878–79. In the second half of the nineteenth century stories and serialized novels in the major journals and magazines regularly received critical comment in newspapers and in other magazines (just as television shows are now widely reviewed, particularly when they premiere). But, as Edmond L. Volpe pointed out in 1958, the periodical literature of 1878–79 shows that *Daisy Miller* was well received; indeed, Volpe was unable to turn up even one review that would seem to bear out the "Contributor's Club" remark on the "critical experts" who had denounced James's best-selling tale.[20] As Leon Edel observed a few years later, "The story . . . was an extraordinary success, but not the *succès de scandale* which legend has attributed to it."[21] We should add, however, that Howells was probably right in suggesting that *Daisy Miller* occasioned intense debate and some outrage in polite American society if not in the columns of the professional literary critics, for his remark that "society almost divided itself into Daisy Millerites and anti-Daisy Millerites" is supported by an editorial that was published in the *New York Times* less than a year after the story came out in the *Cornhill*: "There are many ladies in and around New York today," observed the *Times* editorialist, "who feel very indignant with Mr. James for his portrait of *Daisy Miller,* and declare that it is shameful to give foreigners so untrue a portrait of an American girl."[22]

Generally speaking, contemporary critics praised *Daisy Miller* for its stylistic felicity, its clarity, and its faithful realism. The word "clever" is used repeatedly by the reviewers to describe James's success in the tale. In general, too, their comments show that they recognized his success in achieving the aims that we now understand to be intrinsic to the enterprise of American realists of the period: documentary accuracy implicitly conducive to moral improvement and refinement. As James wrote in "The Art of Fiction" (1884), "The only reason for the existence of a novel is that it does attempt to represent life. . . . as the picture is reality, so the novel is history." The indispensable element for the novelist, James added, is freedom, freedom not to be inhibited by conventional ideas of what is proper, by hidebound notions of what is morally instructive, for "The essence of moral energy is to survey the whole field."[23]

Typical among early reviews was the notice that appeared in the *New York Times*. There we read that "Mr. James has surpassed all of his previous writings for the clearness of his conception and the accuracy of his observations. The tragical sketch of a young girl from Schenectady may not be recognized as a Portrait of any maiden of that old Dutch town. . . . But take her as a type that embraces the characteristics of various young women from America now journeying about Europe . . . and the truth and cleverness of this sketch will appear." James, moreover, is praised for "sincere patriotism, since he consecrates his talents to the enlightening of his countrywomen in the view which cynical Europe takes of the performance of the American girl abroad." The *Times* concludes, "We fail to remember anyone who can write so well balanced and clever a short story as this last by Mr. James." Similarly, the reviewer for the *Nation* praised "that true, clever, painful little story called 'Daisy Miller'" as "the best thing Mr. James has ever done" and as "a perfect study of a type not, alas! uncommon." The *Nation*, too, looked for James's story to have an improving effect on its American readers, expressing the hope that "the American people . . . may see themselves here truthfully portrayed, and may say, 'Not so, but otherwise will we be,'" and remarking that while it might be "hard on Mr. James to make him a moral reformer," "he must console himself with the modern dogma that whatever is clever enough is necessarily moral." Finally, Richard Grant White, writing in the *North American Review,* concurred that James had given "a characteristic portrait of a certain sort of American young woman, who is unfortunately too common," a portrait that is "very faithful," and that "may have some corrective effect."[24] One supposes that James, the champion of artistic freedom, would have found it ironic at least that within a quarter of a century of the publication of *Daisy Miller* the reviewers' suggestions about the possibly "corrective effect" of his tale had been codified in the prescriptions of etiquette books that warned young women to shun the example of Daisy Miller.[25] By that time everyone knew what a "Daisy Miller" was, even if he or she had not read James's tale, just as today we all know what a "Rambo" is even though many of us will never watch one of the films in which Rambo is featured.

The most important early commentators on *Daisy Miller*

were William Dean Howells and Henry James himself. In 1882, in an essay titled "Henry James, Jr.," Howells observed that "so far as the average American girl was studied at all in Daisy Miller, her indestructible innocence, her invulnerable new-worldliness, had never been so delicately appreciated," and Howells praised James for what he suggested was his "most characteristic quality," "the artistic impartiality which puzzled so many in the treatment of Daisy Miller": "As 'frost performs the effect of fire,' this impartiality comes at last to the same result as sympathy."[26] In 1901 Howells devoted a chapter to *Daisy Miller* in his two-volume *Heroines of Fiction*. There he remarked that "The tendency was then [in the period following the Civil War] toward a subtle beauty, which he [James] more than any other American writer has expressed in his form, and toward a keen, humorous, penetrating self-criticism, which seized with joy upon the expanding national life, and made it the material of fiction as truly national as any yet known." Howells saw that in Daisy James was "the inventor, beyond question, of the international American girl," and he observed that James's portrayal of "the innocently adventuring, uncon-sciously periculant American maiden" was so influential that it in effect brought an end to the Daisy Miller type: having seen James's portrayal of Daisy, real American girls would never again behave, innocently and unconsciously, as she had done: "It is a melancholy paradox, but we need not be inconsolable, for though she has perished forever from the world, we have her spiritual reflex still vivid in the sensitive mirror which caught with such accuracy her girlish personality." In addition, Howells praised *Daisy Miller* for its "perfection of workman-ship": "no word could be spared without in some degree spoil-ing it, none could be added without cumbering its beauty with a vain decoration."[27]

Howells's comments are interesting because he offers pen-etrating insights as well as because he is an important American novelist, editor, and man of letters and a lifelong friend of

Henry James. James's comments are even more interesting because they come, as it were, from the horse's mouth. Before we turn to them, however, I want to note that literary criticism long ago passed the point at which we could take an author's comments about his or her work simply at face value. In the 1930s the New Critics pointed out the problems of interpreting works according to their authors' intentions, a form of critical naïveté they called "the intentional fallacy." They helped us to see that in the literary criticism of a practicing poet such as T. S. Eliot we are not reading a hypothetical "disinterested" commentator but, rather, a highly *interested* critic whose comments on, say, Wordsworth have less to do with the romantic poet than with Eliot's effort to justify his own poetry and poetics and to create an audience for his own work. The New Critics also helped us to appreciate that even the greatest author—Shakespeare, for instance, in *Hamlet*—could not have intended all of the meanings that have been intelligently understood to be operating in his work by directors, actors, audiences, general readers, and critics and scholars.[28] In addition, among the most important lessons that we have learned from the new new critics of the last three decades—the modern literary theorists in all of their rich and challenging variety—is that no interpretation is innocent of theory, of some ideological foundation, whether or not the interpreter is conscious of that theoretical groundwork.[29] All interpretations are by definition *interested* (as opposed to *disinterested*), and those promulgated by authors about their own work must therefore be doubly suspect.

James offered two important commentaries on *Daisy Miller*. In the first, a letter of 1880, he assured a correspondent, Eliza Lynn Linton, that "Poor little Daisy Miller was, as I understand her, above all things *innocent*." As James puts the matter in this letter, moreover, Daisy was too innocent ever to "take the measure really of the scandal she produced" and too innocent for one to "suggest that she was playing off Giovanelli against Winterbourne." James dismisses the idea that Daisy was

consciously "defiant" of the conventions of the American expatriate community in Rome. For "she was too ignorant, too
irreflective, too little versed in the proportions of things": "The
whole idea of the story is the little tragedy of a light, thin, natural, unsuspecting creature being sacrificed as it were to a social
rumpus that went on quite over her head and to which she
stood in no measurable relation."[30] James's statements about
Daisy's innocence, combined with Winterbourne's assent to
Giovanelli's affirmation of her innocence at the end of *Daisy
Miller,* would seem to remove any possible doubt on that score.
But readers may reasonably disagree with Henry James about
the extent to which Daisy can be viewed as consciously defiant
of—and critical of—the social system with which she is con-
fronted. As a recent critic observes, the author "was very uneasy
as to the degree of romantic sympathy he had shown for Daisy
in the story, and perhaps his remarks in the letter can be seen
partly as a reaction to this. At any rate, one can only hold to
the way Daisy actually appears to exist in the reading of the
story."[31]

James's second major pronouncement on *Daisy Miller* appeared in 1909 in the preface to volume 18 of the New York
Edition of *The Novels and Tales of Henry James,* the volume
that included his recently and heavily revised version of *Daisy
Miller.* We must remember that James was writing about a revision made some thirty years after the original tale (I say more
about his prefatory remarks later in this book, in a section devoted to the very different, late version). In 1909 James recalled
that the tale had originated in an anecdote told him by a friend
in Rome, about "some simple and uninformed American lady
of the previous winter, whose young daughter, a child of nature
and of freedom, accompanying her from hotel to hotel, had
'picked up' by the wayside, with the best conscience in the
world, a good-looking Roman, of vague identity, astonished at
his luck, yet (so far as might be, by the pair) all serenely exhibited and introduced: this at least till the occurrence of some

small social check, some interrupting incident, of no great gravity and dignity, and which I forget." James heard nothing further of these American ladies, but the anecdote exhorted him to "Dramatise, dramatise!" In the preface, also, James recalls the initial rejection of the story, the theory that it had been taken as an "outrage on American girlhood," and its extraordinary success. He also puts forward a view that seems to most readers more apt for his revision than for the original tale, that Daisy was not realistically portrayed, that she was, rather, "pure poetry, and had never been anything else."[32]

Modern studies of *Daisy Miller* have dealt with a variety of special topics as well as with general interpretations of the story. Among the special topics, in addition to Elizabeth Hoxie's essay and the notes by George Monteiro and Edmund Volpe (see notes 18, 20, and 25), are several essays that deal with James's sources in Continental fiction. Viola Dunbar and Edward Stone discuss parallels in characterization and plot between *Daisy Miller* and Victor Cherbuliez's *Paule Méré*. More recently, Motley F. Deakin has suggested that the heroines of George Sand, Mme De Staël, and Ivan Turgenev, as well as of Cherbuliez, were no less important as models for Daisy Miller than the real American girls James observed. In this essay, incidentally, Deakin reads *Daisy Miller* against the grain of the author's comments in the 1880 letter to Mrs. Linton; Deakin does not emphasize Daisy's innocence but her spirit of independence and rebellion, which makes her "a champion and martyr to freedom."[33] Some attention has also been paid to James's American sources for *Daisy Miller,* particularly in Hawthorne, and I would add that, though James is an extraordinarily different writer from Mark Twain, his Daisy Miller and his other innocent Americans in Europe are cousins, as it were, to the travelers portrayed in Twain's *Innocents Abroad.*[34]

Several studies deal with the significance of James's allusions to Byron and to Velázquez in *Daisy Miller.* Carl Wood argues that Byron's "The Prisoner of Chillon" is a source for

James's tale.[35] More generally, in "*Daisy Miller* and Baedeker" (the first of his "Two Studies of *Daisy Miller*") Motley Deakin provides a telling account of passages by Byron that James's readers would have known well and that concern two key settings in *Daisy Miller,* the Castle of Chillon and the Colosseum; Deakin also explicates the associations (and thus the thematic implications) that all of the settings of the tale would have had for nineteenth-century American travelers and readers of then-popular travel literature.[36] In two essays published almost simultaneously Adeline R. Tintner and Jeffrey Meyers discuss James's ironic posing of Daisy Miller, a true innocent, beneath Velázquez's famous portrait of Pope Innocent X, who, notoriously, was innocent in name only.[37]

There have been several studies of James's revision of *Daisy Miller,* including an article by Viola Dunbar that greatly favors the revised New York Edition text and a dissertation by Dee Hansen Ohi that, in exhaustive detail, makes the consensus case that the earlier version is the superior of the two.[38] Collations of the variants between the early and late versions can be found in an appendix to an essay by W. M. Gibson and G. R. Petty and in the appendix to volume 3 of Maqbool Aziz's edition of *The Tales of Henry James.*[39] Frederick Newberry suggests that James twice inserted the word "horror" into the revised tale so that when Mrs. Costello calls Daisy "a horror" (instead of a "dreadful girl," as in the earlier version), we can imagine that Winterbourne hears "whore."[40] A valuable article by Carol Ohmann also draws on comparisons of the original and revised texts (though Ohmann argues that James's intentions changed in the course of his composition of the original tale and that the change is inscribed in that text).[41] Lauren Cowdery attributes what she sees as the comparative failure of the revised text to the incompatibility of the structure of the original with a subtext that James chose to highlight in seeking to rewrite *Daisy Miller* as a *nouvelle,* a fictional genre "he had only recently come to theorize about." Cowdery's commentary provides, incidentally, one of the most acute and penetrating overviews of the technical and thematic dimensions of *Daisy Miller.* Also of considerable, related interest are the remarks of Mary Doyle Springer in her book-length study of the novella as a literary form.[42]

During the first half of the twentieth century most critics saw Daisy Miller as embodying an ideal or ideals.[43] Since the 1950s, however, two trends have been apparent in criticism of *Daisy Miller.* One is the increasing interest in Winterbourne as the Jamesian "central intelligence" character and even as the hero of the tale. The other is a disposition to see the story as critical of Daisy and of the limitations of American culture as well as of Winterbourne and of the Europeanized values in which he is implicated. Both these trends are admirably surveyed by Richard Hocks in his centennial essay on *Daisy Miller.*[44] The view of Winterbourne as central character received a strong impetus from Wayne C. Booth's commentary in *The Rhetoric of Fiction* (a discussion principally concerned with technique), and it is developed with more thematic emphasis in important essays by James Gargano, John H. Randall, R. P. Draper, Ian Kennedy, William E. Grant, and Cathy N. Davidson.[45] We should note, however, that there is a considerable range of opinion within these representative Winterbourne-centered readings. Kennedy and Davidson, for example, see Winterbourne as having a lively sexual interest in Daisy whereas Gargano reads him as a "morbid latter day Puritan" and Draper reads him as a Prufrock who undergoes a "slow death." The modern view that James was criticizing Daisy as well as the Europeanized Americans found early exponents in F. W. Dupee and in Leon Edel (who argues that James's principal target was the abdication of authority over their children by American parents).[46] Hocks's centennial essay is itself an outstanding example of an interpretation that is persuasively critical of both Daisy and Winterbourne. More recently, in "Poor Daisy, Poor Winterbourne" (the second half of his "Two Studies of Daisy Miller" [see n. 36]) Motley Deakin offers a first-rate discussion that is balanced not so much in its criticism of, but in its sympathy for, the two characters. (Deakin's two-part article, incidentally, was praised by Robert L. Gale in the Henry James chapter of *American Literary Scholarship 1983* [Durham: Duke University Press, 1985] as "the best essay I have ever read on *Daisy Miller.*") William Stafford's collection on *Daisy Miller* includes important cultural analyses of the tale by Leslie Fiedler and Tristram P. Coffin, among others (see n. 18). Finally, it must be said that there are simply too many excellent commentaries on *Daisy Miller* to survey them adequately in a brief chapter. Readers who wish to explore the criticism more fully should consult the bibliographies of James studies by Kristian Pruitt McColgan and Dorothy M. Scura, the annual *MLA International Bibliography,* and the annual bibliographical essays on James studies in *American Literary Scholarship* and in the *Henry James Review.*[47]

A Reading

4

VOICE AND POINT OF VIEW

It should be said at the outset that the experience of reading *Daisy Miller* remains for most readers what it has been since the story came out in the *Cornhill*, a very considerable pleasure. My aim in this series of chapters on reading *Daisy Miller* is to extend and deepen that pleasure by exploring the text from a variety of vantage points—stylistic and technical as well as thematic and historical—in order to make its inner workings and its implications clearer and easier to grasp, particularly for readers coming to Henry James for the first time on the threshold of the twenty-first century. I hope, too, that some of these observations will open up *Daisy Miller* in new ways even for seasoned Jamesians.

James's story may seem at first glance comparatively simple. Comedy flows from the inability of Daisy and Winterbourne, two young Americans with astonishingly different cultural backgrounds and social training, to understand each other. Dramatic tension builds with Winterbourne's fluctuating, inept efforts to classify Daisy, to arrive at "the formula" for her (10), and with Daisy's "ostracism" (43) by the society of expatriate Americans in Rome. Tragedy and pathos—and the sentimental—strike with Daisy's death. And the multiple ironies of the tale are capped by Winterbourne's belated recognitions that Daisy was "innocent" and that, had he offered her his love, she would have returned it; as he puts it in his comically stiff way, "[s]he would have appreciated one's esteem" (49). *Daisy Miller* combines incisive realism about American manners in the mid-1870s with the creation, in Daisy herself, of a prototypical myth of innocent American girlhood, a creation that the author would look back on long afterwards as "pure poetry."

But, of course, we quickly notice that any such attempt to sum up the "simple" elements of *Daisy Miller* betrays itself by the complex clash of opposing terms it entails: James's story is such that it forces us to yoke together comedy and tragedy, sentimentality and irony, realism and mythmaking. Our experience of the story, I believe, is that these yokings together are not difficult or violent. They are, rather, achieved with apparent ease and with an effect of serenity in large part because of James's accomplished command of narrative and because of his dazzling verbal facility, attributes of his genius that were very much in evidence at this early stage in his artistic career. To these multifaceted elements, James's narrative technique and his style in *Daisy Miller,* I devote this chapter.

We hear, first of all, a range of voices in *Daisy Miller.* Native to the three Millers—Daisy, her mother, and her brother Randolph—is an unvarnished, colloquial American speech. "My sister ain't the best!" Randolph exclaims. "She's always blowing at me" (5). Daisy says of her mother, "[s]he don't like to ride round in the afternoon" (11). She calls Mrs. Miller "right down timid" (17). She tells Winterbourne that she had feared that Rome would be "awfully poky" (30). The homespun grammar and unpolished diction smack of the American frontier; we should recall that the Millers hail from provincial Schenectady in an era when even in Manhattan, the center of the nation's greatest city, most streets were unpaved, most families were without indoor bathrooms, and stray chickens wandered the side streets while goats and pigs rooted in filthy gutters. The voices of the Millers contrast strongly with the voices of the Europeanized American matrons, Mrs. Costello and Mrs. Walker: compare virtually any speech of Daisy's with Mrs. Walker's "*Elle s'affiche* [she flaunts her impropriety]. It's her revenge for my having ventured to remonstrate with her" (37). Daisy would never offer a pronouncement in French, nor would she "venture to remonstrate" with anyone. And since the central conflict in the story revolves around Daisy and Winterbourne's mutual incomprehension, James makes the most of the contrast between her vernacular speech and his elaborate, formal diction. Thus, for example, James follows Winterbourne's question, "Your brother is not interested in ancient monuments?" with Daisy's affirmative translation of Winterbourne's terms into her own lingo: "He says he don't care much about old castles" (11). The clash of styles of speaking is telling and deliciously comic.

Beyond the voices of the characters, however, there is a pervasive, commanding voice, that of the authorial presence, a voice that is not quite Henry James's but that resembles his and that more properly belongs to the persona of the narrator he has created for this tale (a narrator much like those of James's other works of this period). This narrator is urbane, sophisticated, ironical. He is highly knowledgeable about European and American manners, about the places he describes, about the monuments and works of art of Europe, and, in short, about all of the accoutrements of high civilization. He is a shrewd and close observer. He takes considerable delight in his own way with words, and we find ourselves taking pleasure in his facility, not least of all when it is used to satiric effect. He is given to epithets that recur with satiric force, notably in the twenty-three repetitions of the adjective *little* to describe Daisy herself.[48]

We are introduced to this urbane Jamesian narrator in the polished first paragraph of the tale. "At the little town of Vevey, in Switzerland, there is a particularly comfortable hotel" (3): reading this, we know already that we are in the hands of a connoisseur of European travel, one who knows the little towns as well as the great cities and who has a sufficiently wide experience to discriminate between a *particularly* comfortable hotel and others that are satisfactory but not superlative. Thus, in a single sentence, James's narrator makes a powerful implicit assertion of his authority and reliability and a strong bid, consequently, for the reader's trust. The voice that proceeds throughout the opening paragraph is marvelously nuanced. In the second sentence, for example, when the narrator says that Vevey is "seated upon the edge of a remarkably blue lake," we simultaneously imagine the unusual blueness of the lake and detect in the narrator's "remarkably" an arch, amused condescension to the touristic claims—to what today we might call the "hype"—of the prosperous resort he is describing. It is as though, with the slightest hint of a wink or the least tilt of his head, the speaker, having established his authority, has now taken us into his confidence, has invited us to share in his sophisticated appreciation of a scene in which he has everything placed, pegged, and displayed for comparative evaluation. The language here is that of informative travel writing, one sure sign of which is the use, in the first paragraph, of the present tense— "there *is* a particularly comfortable hotel," "the shore of the lake *presents* an unbroken array of establishments," "in the month of June, American travelers *are* extremely numerous," and so on (3). By contrast, the narrative voice modulates in the second paragraph into the characteristic past tense of storytelling: "It was a beautiful summer morning," "He had come from Geneva the day before," "He was some seven-and-twenty years of age," and so on (4).

The first paragraph, moreover (and not to get ahead of ourselves), is remarkably economical and efficient. In moving rapidly to describe the similarities and differences between Vevey and such famed American resorts of the day as Newport and

Saratoga, the narrator introduces the central contrast of the tale, the opposition of American and European culture and manners. Every detail with which the narrator develops this international theme, moreover, is carefully selected for what it foreshadows. The "flitting hither and thither of 'stylish' young girls, a rustling of muslin flounces, a rattle of dance-music in the morning, a sound of high-pitched voices at all times"—the details that support the observation that Vevey has "sights and sounds which evoke a vision, an echo, of Newport and Saratoga"—all forecast Daisy herself, with her wonderful vitality, her stylish dressing "in perfection" (13), her "white muslin, with a hundred frills and flounces" (5), her chattering—"the most charming garrulity he [Winterbourne] had ever heard" (22)—and her love of dancing. Each of the "other features that are much at variance" with the suggestions in Vevey of an American resort is selected for the resonance it will develop as the story progresses. The description of "neat German waiters, who look like secretaries of legation" anticipates Mrs. Costello's imputation that the Millers are overly familiar with their courier (a servant in charge of traveling arrangements) because "they have never seen a man with such good manners, such fine clothes, so like a gentleman" (14) and her later observation that Daisy believes Giovanelli to be "the most elegant man in the world, the finest gentleman. . . . he is better even than the courier" (41). The detail of "Russian princesses sitting in the garden" anticipates Winterbourne's observation that Daisy had "the *tournure* [manner or bearing] of a princess" (12). The notation of "little Polish boys walking about, held by the hand, with their governors" anticipates, in implicit contrast, the unsupervised, ungoverned—and in fact ungovernable—little American boy, Randolph Miller, and Daisy's statement that Randolph hasn't "got any boys here. There is only one boy here, but he always goes around with a teacher; they won't let him play" (8). Finally, the detail with which the first paragraph closes, "a view of the snowy crest of the Dent du Midi and the picturesque towers of the Castle of Chillon," anticipates the excursion Daisy and Winterbourne will take to the castle and their later travels, across the mountains to the south (of which the Dent du Midi is one), to Italy. Every element in the paragraph, in short, is working to good effect, bearing out Howells's observation that "no word could be spared without in some degree spoiling it."[49]

Having accomplished so much so economically in the first paragraph, the present-tense travel-authority narrator nearly disappears from the story thereafter, making just one more brief appearance in the description of the Pincian Garden (see the first two sentences in the last paragraph beginning on p. 35). For with the shift from present to past tense in the second paragraph of *Daisy Miller* comes a highly significant change in the perspective of the narrator. Still amused, still sophisticated, still condescending, and still a dazzling phrase-maker, he now becomes a limited omniscient narrator, limited, crucially, by Winterbourne's point of view. From the moment that Winterbourne is introduced—introduced, we should note, as someone not completely an open book to the narrator, who brings Winterbourne on with the words "I hardly know whether it was the analogies or the differences that were uppermost in the mind of a young American, who . . ." (3–4)—he functions as the center of consciousness in the story. That is, what is narrated thereafter is told from Winterbourne's point of view. Sometimes the narrator records in the third-person words that almost seem transcriptions of Winterbourne's thoughts, as in the following passage recording Winterbourne's perplexity in the course of his first encounter with Daisy:

> Certainly she was very charming, but how deucedly sociable! Was she simply a pretty girl from New York State—were they all like that, the pretty girls who had a good deal of gentlemen's society? Or was she also a designing, an audacious, an unscrupulous young person? Winterbourne had lost his instinct in this matter, and his reason could not help him. Miss Daisy Miller looked extremely

> innocent. Some people had told him that, after all, American girls
> were exceedingly innocent; and others had told him that, after all,
> they were not. He was inclined to think that Miss Daisy Miller
> was a flirt—a pretty American flirt. . . . Winterbourne was almost
> grateful for having found the formula that applied to Miss Daisy
> Miller. (10)

Here much of the phrasing is clearly Winterbourne's own way
of putting matters to himself, including the appellation "Miss
Daisy Miller," the exclamation "how deucedly sociable," and,
most decisively, the phrase "a pretty American flirt," the very
"formula" that Winterbourne is relieved to have found. With
such third-person representations of his character's thoughts
James is applying a literary technique he learned from his reading of Gustave Flaubert, the indirect free style (or, in French, *le
style indirect libre*). The technique is used widely, for instance,
in Flaubert's *Madame Bovary*; a few years after *Daisy Miller*
James would bring it to perfection in chapter 42 of *The Portrait
of a Lady*, a long third-person account of his heroine's medita-
tion on her failed marriage that is often taken as the most
notable forecast in nineteenth-century fiction in English of
twentieth-century stream-of-consciousness narration.

Much of the time, however, the narrator is somewhat more
distant from Winterbourne than such near-transcriptions of the
character's thoughts would suggest. Occasionally, the narrator's
language tells us that he does not know Winterbourne's
thoughts and feelings but is merely conjecturing them; for example, just after introducing Winterbourne, he says, "in whatever fashion the young American looked at things, they must
have seemed to him charming" (4). Sometimes he subtly implies
criticism of Winterbourne. When we read, "But his aunt had a
headache—his aunt had almost always a headache—and now
she was shut up in her room, smelling camphor, so that he was
at liberty to wander about" (4), the clause "so that he was at
liberty to wander about" implies that Winterbourne is very
much under his aunt's thumb, and this points to one aspect of

his weakness, his subservience to the women in his life. This subservience is exemplified by his attendance on his aunt, by his need, at the end of the second section of the story, to return to his mistress in Geneva, and by his compliance with Mrs. Walker's dictates in the big dramatic scene at the Pincio in the third section. Sometimes the narrator condescends to Winterbourne, as when he calls him "Poor Winterbourne" (23) in amusement and mock sympathy with his bewilderment and insensitivity. And now and then the narrator suggests outright contempt for Winterbourne, as the word *derisive* in the following sentence suggests: "At the risk of exciting a somewhat derisive smile on the reader's part, I may affirm that with regard to the women who had hitherto interested him it very often seemed to Winterbourne among the possibilities that, given certain contingencies, he should be afraid—literally afraid—of these ladies" (40).

I do not mean to suggest that the narrator views Winterbourne with derision, that that is his "true" attitude toward the character, and that everything else is a subterfuge. My point, rather, is that the narrator's perspective on Winterbourne entails a very complex blend of sympathy and criticism, empathy and analysis, closeness and distance. Sympathy, empathy, and closeness are essential since Winterbourne *is* the point-of-view character; after the first paragraph, he provides the point of vantage on everything that happens in *Daisy Miller*. But criticism, analysis, and distance are also essential because James's story exposes Winterbourne's limitations even more than it exposes Daisy's. There is, indeed, masterful brilliance in the way in which, at times, James allows his narrator to express sympathy and admiration for Winterbourne in contexts that are finally devastating to him. When Winterbourne takes Daisy to the Castle of Chillon, for example, he is preoccupied with his sexual fantasies of forbidden intimacy with her—much more about this point later. Particularly when we are rereading the story, however, we know that Daisy is innocent, that on the occasion of the excursion to Chillon she has not the least thought of illicit pleasures, and that she is simply doing what she appears to be doing, enjoying the outing. Here is the narrator's observation on Winterbourne as Daisy comes down to join him in the hotel lobby for the excursion to Chillon: "Winterbourne was a man of imagination and, as our ancestors used to say, of sensibility; as he looked at her dress and, on the great staircase, her little rapid, confiding step, he felt as if there was something romantic going forward. He could have believed he was going to elope with her" (21). Ironically, even as the narrator praises Winterbourne for imagination and sensibility, we can see that the story is in large part about the failure of these very qualities in him; not only is his imagination incapable of encompassing Daisy's true innocence, but it is also engaged in sexually brutalizing her while she innocently chatters away, and his vaunted sensibility is really, in the very episode in which the term is used, an insensitivity to Daisy's genuine nature. In dreaming of elopement with Daisy, Winterbourne, the man of so-called imagination and sensibility, has his companion all wrong.

The narrator's treatment of the other characters is necessarily quite different from the way he handles Winterbourne. No one else provides the point of view; everyone else is observed externally. We know Mrs. Costello and Mrs. Walker, we know Eugenio and Giovanelli, above all we know Daisy Miller herself from what they do and say, from what we hear others say about them, and from Winterbourne's thoughts about them (interpreted with due regard for his frequent confusion and mistakes). Although we come, like Giovanelli, like Winterbourne, and like Henry James himself, to believe in Daisy Miller's innocence, we are never privy to her thoughts. Poignantly, the closest we come to knowing her from the inside is in the glimpses Winterbourne has of her pain, first when she realizes that Mrs. Costello declines to meet her and declares "You needn't be afraid! I'm not afraid!" with "a little laugh" that leads Winterbourne to fancy that "there was a tremor in her voice" (16) and then, later, when he realizes from her paleness after Mrs. Walker turns her back on her that Daisy "was too much shocked and puzzled even for indignation" (39). Usually, however, we do not come even this close to Daisy's inner life. She is shown to us, rather, in dramatic passages in which the narrator almost abandons Winterbourne's point of view and becomes, as Deakin puts it, "only an eye and an ear and a recording memory." Much of Winterbourne's first encounter with Randolph and Daisy Miller is such an objective recording, though Winterbourne's thoughts ("Winterbourne had immediately perceived . . . ," "Winterbourne wondered . . . ," "'How pretty they are!' thought Winterbourne" [5–6]) are regularly interpolated. For, as Deakin also remarks, "having already established his other authorial roles, James can slip out of this neutrality whenever he wishes without too obvious an interruption of the fictive illusion."[50]

Later in his career Henry James would make the limiting of point of view to a single character a central precept of his theory of fiction. He would call such a point-of-view character his "center of consciousness," or his "central intelligence," or a "lucid reflector." This last term indicated his view that success for him lay in choosing a central intelligence who is unusually intelligent, observant, and sensitive and who is therefore as fine a register as possible for the human, psychological drama seen through his eyes. At the same time, such a character should not be infallible; indeed, the very errors of vision and understanding of the central-intelligence character would be the source of drama and conflict in James's fiction. Perhaps the closest James came to an ideal realization of this theory in his own fiction is in Lambert Strether in *The Ambassadors* (1903). So far as the theory of fiction is concerned, the idea of the supreme importance of point of view has come to be closely linked to Henry James.

For this very reason we need to be on guard against reading the 1878 *Daisy Miller* back through James's later theory and through his later fiction, need to be on guard, above all, against mistaking Winterbourne for the kind of viewpoint character we find in Strether. For one thing, as already indicated, Winter-bourne is insensitive and imperceptive to a degree that makes him culpable far beyond Strether's generous mistakes of percep-tion. In addition, James's method in *Daisy Miller: A Study* is much less rigorously and systematically bound by the perspec-tive of his point-of-view character than it would be later on. For example, in *The Ambassadors,* when James wants us to know that Strether is the editor of a literary and intellectual quarterly, he has Strether convey this data in dialogue with another char-acter, Maria Gostrey, whereas when the narrator of *Daisy Miller* wants us to know that Winterbourne has a mistress in Geneva he intrusively and omnisciently informs us of what those who know Winterbourne have to say on the matter: "when his friends spoke of him, they usually said that he was at Geneva 'studying' . . . when certain persons spoke of him they affirmed that the reason of his spending so much time at Geneva was that he was extremely devoted to a lady who lived there" (4). Similarly, the narrator makes highly critical com-ments on Winterbourne that are external to his point of view, such as the one we have recently noted that begins "At the risk of exciting a somewhat derisive smile on the reader's part . . ." (40). What we can say about Winterbourne in relation to James's later practice is that in this character James works with a method, and develops a character, that would have to be judged highly flawed by the standards of the later theory, or that, alternatively, looks forward only in some limited respects to what would come later; but we should also add that there is little to be gained in holding up this early work against James's later theory and practice except to highlight differences between the early and late James. Winterbourne is less a prototype for Lambert Strether, the nearly ideal fulfillment of late Jamesian theory, than for the deeply flawed protagonists of some of James's late shorter fictions, notably John Marcher in "The Beast in the Jungle," who shares Winterbourne's emotional coldness and blinding self-regard.

One of the sources of our pleasure in reading *Daisy Miller,* finally, is the narrator's exuberant felicity with language. Generally, this happy talent for phrasemaking is used to humorous effect. A few examples should suffice to illustrate the point. After Randolph declares, "My father ain't in Europe; my father's in a better place than Europe," we enjoy the ironic deflation of Winterbourne's quaintly euphemistic and elaborately formal speculation "that this was the manner in which the child had been taught to intimate that Mr. Miller had been removed to the sphere of celestial rewards" by Randolph's immediate addition, "My father's in Schenectady. He's got a big business. My father's rich, you bet" (8). The narrator is delightfully satiric in his description of Mrs. Costello, "who frequently intimated that, if she were not so dreadfully liable to sick-headaches, she would probably have left a deeper impress upon her time" (13). Mrs. Costello's headaches are balanced by Mrs. Miller's dyspepsia and "pathological gossip" (27). The account of Winterbourne's vision of Daisy "surrounded by half-a-dozen wonderful moustaches" is another characteristic example of the narrator's turns of phrase being a source of interest and of pleasure for the reader. Not all such turns, of course, are used to comic effect. The description of Daisy's grave as a "raw protuberance among the April daisies" is memorable and affecting (49). So is the change the narrator effects in the connotations of the word *poor* between the scene in St. Peter's in which, among "Mrs. Costello and her friends, there was a great deal said about poor little Miss Miller's going really 'too far'" (42) and the report a few pages later that "[a] week after this the poor girl died" (49). Comic or not, such language, as Deakin says, is intended "to elicit pleasure and satisfaction as much from the verbal ingenuity displayed as from the information it may provide."[51]

As I indicated in the first note to this chapter (n. 48), my discussion here is deeply indebted to Professor Deakin's excellent recent commentary on *Daisy Miller*. I have been careful, nevertheless, to speak of the "narrator" where Deakin speaks of the "author" in the belief that the narrator is not Henry James but a fictional creation, a persona, a voice invented by the author in order to accomplish specific tasks within the artifice that is *Daisy Miller*.[52] The author, on the other hand, has priority (and control) over the narrator. It is the author, moreover, who decides the events he will have the narrator relate, who determines not only what happens but also when, who selects the names of the characters, determines the settings of the tale, and so on. It is to such matters of authorial decision, particularly names, settings, and times, that I turn in the next chapter.

5

TIMES, NAMES, PLACES, SYMBOLS

The successful fusion of literary realism and of mythmaking in *Daisy Miller* depends in large part on James's skillful use of elements that operate at one and the same time realistically and symbolically. When James avows in his 1909 preface to the revised tale that "my supposedly typical little figure was of course pure poetry, and had never been anything else," he does not do justice to the realism in his depiction of Daisy to which numerous contemporary readers testified; rather, he highlights a poetic, symbolic—even, perhaps, allegorical—dimension that the story always had and that he made primary in the revision. In the original it operated as "only a subtext," as Lauren Cowdery suggests, though it is undoubtedly an important and effective one.[53]

The poetic, mythic dimension of *Daisy Miller* is conveyed, first of all, in the names of the characters. The name *Daisy* suggests Daisy's American naturalness and innocence. Etymologically, *daisy* means "the day's eye," suggesting Daisy's radiance, her fresh, "morning" quality, and beautifully fitting into the further symbolism that flowerlike Daisy closes up and then dies after Winterbourne cuts her ("He saw me—and he cuts me!" Daisy exclaims [46]) at night in the Colosseum. Her status as flower dovetails also with Winterbourne's first meeting her in the garden of his hotel in Vevey, with his walking with her later in the Pincian Garden in Rome, with his encountering her thereafter "in that beautiful abode of flowering desolation known as the Palace of the Caesars" (43), and with his final view of her grave, that "raw protuberance among the April daisies" (49). Since James calls Daisy's real-life prototype in the anecdote that was the germ of *Daisy Miller* "a child of nature and freedom," it is appropriate that Daisy be named for a flower common in the wild in her native North America.[54] Commonness, moreover, is suggested by her surname, *Miller,* a name derived from a trade, the grinding of grain. James uses Mrs. Costello to emphasize the proletarian ordinariness of the name *Miller* when he has her fumble a moment for it, referring to "that young lady's—Miss Baker's, Miss Chandler's [a chandler is one who makes or sells candles]—what's her name?—Miss Miller's intrigue" (40). On the other hand, to return to Daisy's first name, since the mid-eighteenth-century *daisy* has been American slang for "any excellent, remarkable, or admirable person or thing; a choice specimen; a honey," for "a pretty girl," and also for "a grave, death" (from the expression "pushing up daisies").[55] Theodore Dreiser uses the term in the second sense ("a pretty girl") when he has Drouet greet Carrie Meeber on a Chicago street with the words, "You're a daisy."[56] Clearly the first two slang meanings apply to, and compliment, Daisy, while the third ("a grave, death") is resonant with the daisies by her grave in the Protestant Cemetery at the end of the story.

The symbolic suggestiveness of *Frederick Winterbourne* lies chiefly in the surname. *Winter* suggests coldness and the death of vegetation. Winterbourne's rigidity and his frosty treatment of Daisy in the Colosseum when he believes she has shown herself to be disreputable chill her, eliciting her exclamation, "I don't care . . . whether I have Roman fever or not" (48), after which she promptly succumbs to the disease. To be sure, Daisy dies of malaria, but symbolically Winterbourne is the frost that kills the flower; his naked disapproval of Daisy at their last meeting saps her will to live ("I don't care . . ."). *Winterborne* is listed in the *New Dictionary of American Family Names* as meaning "[o]ne who came from Winterborne (stream dry except in winter), the name of several places in England."[57] In adding a *u* to the name, however (Winterbo*u*rne), James suggests not only the etymology "winter / stream" but also reminds us of the most famous use of the term *bourn* in English, Hamlet's description of death in his "to be or not to be" soliloquy as "The undiscovered country, from whose bourn / No traveller returns" (*Hamlet*, 3.1.79–80). Not only does this allusion reinforce the association of Winterbourne with death but also, since *bourn* in Hamlet's speech means "a limit, boundary, or border," it suggests that Winterbourne is limited, that his conformity and his low emotional temperature circumscribe his capacity for life and for love, thus reducing his humanity as well as his imagination.

As for *Frederick,* I confess that I detect less that is suggestive here, though the etymology of the name, "peace/rule" (sometimes glossed as "peaceful ruler"), may imply a certain passivity in his character and a tendency to submit to rule by others. More interesting, I think, is the middle name that James gave Winterbourne in the New York Edition text (he does not have one in the original). In the 1909 version, when Daisy introduces him to her mother, she pronounces his name: "Mr. Frederick Forsyth Winterbourne."[58] *Forsyth* might, I suppose, suggest ironically the failures of insight and of foresight that Winterbourne comes to regret in himself by the end of the story, or it might suggest that he is the scythe that cuts Daisy Miller down. More plausible, I think, would be an inference that the name suggests a flower, forsythia, whereby James meant to indicate some of the common ground Daisy and Winterbourne might have shared if they had only met each other halfway, if she had been a little more formal and conformable and if he had been a little less stiff. Perhaps in the end they are both flowers blighted by the chill of convention; perhaps Winterbourne had it in him, if he had only broken through his reserve and his rigid sense of propriety, to be, like his countrywoman, a child of nature and of freedom.

The other names in the story are not so suggestive. It is hard to make anything of *Costello,* an Irish surname meaning one who is like a fawn or deer, unless it be an ironic comment on the most unfawnlike Mrs. Costello. Mrs. Walker's name might also have ironic implications since she exhorts Daisy not to walk about publicly with Giovanelli; underlying the horror of Daisy's walking the streets is the unexpressed Victorian fear that there is no middle ground for women between unimpeachable propriety and the disrepute of streetwalkers. *Eugenio,* etymologically "well-born," also could be read as ironic. *Giovanelli,* finally, may suggest youth or youthfulness (the single *n* suggests that the name derives from the Italian word *giovane,* a youth, and not from Giova*nn*i, Italian for John). But I would not press any of these possible interpretations. I would observe, nevertheless, that James surely intended the names of his two main characters to have symbolic resonance; he uses names symbolically throughout his fiction, from Christopher Newman, the new man of democratic North America, in *The American* (1877), to Bessie Alden, given the quintessentially American surname of one of the heroic figures of Plymouth Bay (John Alden) in "An International Episode" (1879), to Adam Verver, whose name suggests the primal innocence of Eden, Adam's green (French *vert*) home, in *The Golden Bowl* (1904).

The settings of the story also have rich symbolic implications; in order to appreciate those implications we must take some account of the associations Geneva, Vevey, Chillon, and Rome would have had for readers in 1878–79. The period after the Civil War was one of unprecedented European travel by Americans to rediscover the civilization of the Old World and to experience its pleasures. They were, by and large, far more literate than Americans today, making their transatlantic excursions scarcely more than a generation after Alexis de Tocqueville had observed that there was not a cabin in the American wilderness without its copy of the works of Shakespeare. They went to Europe in search of the picturesque, the romantic, and their expectations were largely shaped by the most popular literature of the nineteenth-century, the great works of English and European romanticism that had cast over the locales of *Daisy Miller*—Lake Geneva, Vevey, the Castle of Chillon, the Roman Pincio, the Colosseum, the Palatine Hill, the Protestant Cemetery where Shelley and Keats lie buried—an aura of mysterious fable, ineffable beauty, and stirring heroism. Before they saw any of these places, the nineteenth-century American (and English) tourist had become familiar with them through the works of Rousseau, Madame de Staël, Goethe, Keats, Shelley, and, above all, Byron. More recently, the Roman scene in particular had been made vivid to English-speaking travelers by its use as the setting of Hawthorne's novel *The Marble Faun* (1860). Every place tourists went had stories associated with it that were ingrained in the popular imagination. And in case these stories were not fresh in mind, the guidebooks that were indispensable companions of even the most seasoned travelers were sure to offer cultivated prods to memory.

Let us consider briefly, for example, some of the notations on Vevey and Chillon in the eighth edition of Baedeker's *Switzerland* (1879). (Guidebooks issued by the German firm Karl Baedeker were the most widely used in the great age of travel of the second half of the nineteenth-century; also popular were *Murray's Handbook: Rome and Its Environs* [1858] and Augustus Hare's guidebooks, notably his *Walks in Rome* [1871], not to mention books of essays on their European travels by such literary figures as Nathaniel Hawthorne, William Dean Howells, and Henry James himself.) Here are the second and third sentences of the Baedeker entry on Vevey: "Rousseau has contributed greatly to immortalise this spot. The views from the small terrace by the market, the quay, and the new *Château de M. Couvreu* (beautiful ˚Garden with exotic plants, fee 1 fr.) embrace the whole scene of the '*Nouvelle Héloïse*,' the 'burning pages' of which accurately depict this lovely neighbourhood."[59] The Baedeker entry on the Castle of Chillon features this quotation from Byron's "Sonnet on Chillon" (the sonnet, which begins "Eternal spirit of the chainless Mind! / Brightest in dungeons, Liberty! thou art / For there thy habitation is the heart," was written by Byron after further information on the Swiss patriot Bonivard convinced him that, in his longer poem "The Prisoner of Chillon," he should have done more to celebrate the hero's "courage and his virtues"):

> Chillon! thy prison is a holy place,
> And thy sad floor an altar,—for 'twas trod,
> Until his very steps have left a trace,
> Worn, as if the cold pavement were a sod,
> By Bonivard!—may none these marks efface,
> For they appeal from tyranny to God.[60]

When Winterbourne escorts Daisy to Chillon, he tells her, "the history of the unhappy Bonivard," and she exclaims "Well; I hope you know enough! . . . I never saw a man that knew so much!" whereupon the narrator observes that the "history of Bonivard had evidently, as they say, gone into one ear and out of the other" (23).

Visiting Chillon, James himself had Baedeker "in hand"—yes, even Henry James, who, like Winterbourne, had been schooled in Geneva, and who had by his mid-thirties spent much of his life in Europe. Here is James on Chillon in "Swiss Notes," an essay from the second of the nearly eighty books he would publish in his lifetime, *Transatlantic Sketches* (1875):

> Temple Bar [in London] itself witnesses a scarcely busier coming and going than, in these days, those hoary portals of Chillon. My own imagination, on experiment, proved too poor an alchemist, and such enjoyment as I got of the castle was mainly my distant

daily view of it from the garden of the Hôtel Byron,—a little, many-pinnacled white promontory, shining against the blue lake. When I went, Bädeker in hand, to "do" the place, I found a huge concourse of visitors awaiting the reflux of an earlier wave. "Let us at least wait till there is no one else," I said to my companion. She smiled in compassion of my naïveté, *There is never no one else*," she answered. "We must treat it as a crush or leave it alone."[61]

That Chillon was never anything but a crush, incidentally, suggests how very "generous" Winterbourne must have been in arranging matters with the custodian of the castle so that he and Daisy could "linger and pause" there, left "quite to themselves" (23).

James clearly chose the setting of Chillon because of its status as a shrine to freedom, consecrated by Byron, whose name (along with those of Victor Hugo and of other heroes of the romantic movement) was scratched into one of the pillars of the castle. The reader's reminiscence of Bonivard's hardy and steadfast espousal of liberty against the tyrannical Duke of Savoy would underline Daisy's spirit of independence and at the same time comment ironically on Winterbourne's timid subservience to social restraints. The association of the Vevey district with Rousseau's once wildly popular epistolary novel, *Julie, ou La Nouvelle Héloïse*, also served James's purpose since the reader was thereby invited to contrast the barely restrainable and eventually consummated passion of Rousseau's hero and heroine with Daisy's innocent chastity and with Winterbourne's low emotional temperature; the reader would also be reminded that Rousseau's central theme in *La Nouvelle Héloïse* is the conflict between individual desire and the restraining codes of society, an apt parallel to the conflict between Daisy's American habits of free social intercourse and the elaborately regulated code of manners she runs up against in Europe. James would have been aware of a further association of Vevey with the spirit of rebellion and liberty; as Baedeker reports, the Church of St.

Martin there contains the remains of some of the Englishmen responsible for the execution of the English King Charles I. Baedeker gives this inscription from the memorial tablet of one of the regicides in the church: *"potestatis arbitrariae oppugnator acerrimus,"* that is, the most passionate opponent of arbitrary power. Baedeker also reports that after the restoration Charles II "demanded the extradition of the refugees, a request with which the Swiss government firmly refused to comply."[62] Nineteenth-century readers, finally, would have found this firm refusal thoroughly in keeping with Switzerland's reputation for hardy independence, associated with the standing of the country as the most ancient republic in Europe and with such national heroes as William Tell, known throughout the English-speaking world, like Bonivard, as a champion of liberty.

Vevey and Chillon, therefore, are settings that contribute to the aura of free-spirited independence that surrounds Daisy. Winterbourne, too, feels liberated at Vevey. As a fashionable resort, the place has for him a gaiety and freedom that contrast with the constrictions of the city from which he has come, Geneva. James's narrator refers to Winterbourne's home base there as "the little metropolis of Calvinism," and lest we miss the implication that Geneva is a center of straitlaced Puritanism, he tells us later that Winterbourne silently contrasted Mrs. Miller's lax supervision of Daisy with the "very different type of maternity . . . of the vigilant matrons who massed themselves in the forefront of social intercourse in the dark old city at the other end of the lake" (19). The Puritanism of Geneva, to which Winterbourne is so accustomed that he has "become dishabituated to the American tone" of girls of Daisy's type (10), would seem to underlie his own fastidiousness about manners and proper appearances, though even he finds his aunt's description of "the minutely hierarchical constitution of the society" of New York City "almost oppressively striking" (13).

The Roman settings of *Daisy Miller* were perhaps even more familiar to contemporary readers of Henry James than the

Swiss. The Pincio (pronounced Pinch-ee-oh) Garden was well known to tourists as a hillside promenade affording magnificent views of Rome. As a late nineteenth-century Baedeker for Central Italy describes it, the Pincio "is a fashionable resort in the evening, about 2 hrs. before sunset, when the military band plays; the Italians then pay and receive visits in their carriages, presenting a gay and characteristic scene."[63] Two other descriptions of the Pincio may further serve to give the flavor of the place. The first is from a travel book on Italy of 1876:

> In the Pincio there is "scarcely room to swing a cat." Yet hundreds of vehicles of every description are dashing or creeping upon one another. . . . But the Romans have little leisure or inclination to bestow a glance upon the gorgeous sight [of the sunset] of which a stranger's eye never tires. They have enough to do to look at objects nearer and dearer to man's eyes than all inanimate things. The princely equipages of the Papal families are all drawn up in the central avenue, near the music-stand, jammed together as in the Hyde Park "Ladies' Mile." Every carriage has its bouquet of lovely women, and at the doors of each, on either side, gallant cavaliers cluster like bees."[64]

The second is from Henry James's "From a Roman Note-Book," another chapter in the 1875 *Transatlantic Sketches*:

> The weather perfect and the crowd (especially to-day) amazing. Such a staring, lounging, dandified, amiable crowd! Who does the vulgar, stay-at-home work of Rome? All the grandees and half the foreigners are there in their carriages. . . . Europe is certainly the continent of *staring*. The ladies on the Pincio have to run the gantlet; but they seem to do so complacently enough. The European woman is brought up to the sense of having a definite part (in the way of manners) to play in public. To lie back in a barouche alone, balancing a parasol, and seeming to ignore the extremely immediate gaze of two serried ranks of male creatures on each side of her path, save here and there to recognize one of them with an imperceptible nod, is one of her daily duties. The number of young men here who lead a purely contemplative life is enormous. They

muster in especial force on the Pincio. . . . The Pincio has a great charm; it is a great resource. I am forever being reminded of the "aesthetic luxury" . . . of living in Rome.[65]

We note in light of these descriptions that Daisy Miller fails to do as the Romans do, both in the minor matter of bestowing her interest on the sunset rather than on the human scene (36) and in the more momentous matter of brazenly walking with a gentleman rather than modestly offering him no more than "an imperceptible nod" from the security of a carriage.

The most famous landmark of Rome is the ruin of the ancient Roman arena, the Colosseum, scene of gladiatorial combats and of naval battles, scene, too, of the martyrdom of Christians sacrificed to wild beasts. It is here that James set the climactic scene of his story, again, as at Chillon, amid Byronic echoes, for Winterbourne murmurs to himself "Byron's famous lines, out of 'Manfred'" (46), lines that concern "the silent worship of the great of old."[66] As Carl Maves points out, however, Winterbourne may well have had in mind the long passage on the Colosseum in Byron's immensely popular *Childe Harold's Pilgrimage*. Here Byron emphasizes it as a place of murderous sacrifice of human life to capricious laws. Byron describes, for instance, a gladiator brought captive to Rome from his native Germany, who dies thinking of "his rude hut by the Danube": "*There* were his young barbarians all at play, / *There* was their Dacian mother—he, their sire, / Butcher'd to make a Roman holiday."[67] James wants us to think, in any case, of the Colosseum as a place of martyrdoms, for he uses the dialogue to cast Daisy as martyr and Winterbourne as murderous lion: "Well," Daisy says to Giovanelli, "he looks at us as one of the old lions or tigers may have looked at the Christian martyrs" (46).

Motley Deakin comments tellingly on the symbolic consistency of the settings in Vevey and in Rome: "When Switzerland is the scene, one finds . . . the . . . struggle of the freedom-loving individual against a callous, oppressive authority. The Roman scene evokes the same rebellious individual, but places him in the presence of what was once a great, magnificent, overwhelming, corruptive power."[68] If such individuals, the Christian martyrs who died for religious conscience, are evoked by the Colosseum, the romantic valorization of the individual and of individual liberty is also suggested by Daisy's final resting place, the Protestant Cemetery in Rome. This site was particularly known to English-speaking readers for containing the graves of two of the major romantic poets, John Keats and Percy Bysshe Shelley, both of whom, like Daisy, died young, and far from home. Shelley, like Byron, wrote poetry passionate in its advocacy of personal and political liberty. As Deakin observes, the Protestant Cemetery is "fitting for those who 'protest,'" like Daisy and Shelley, and it is "hemmed in by an old, imperial Roman wall equally symbolic of the forces the rebel confronts."[69]

Much more might be said about the symbolism of place in *Daisy Miller*. As I suggested in my remarks on Daisy's name, her frequent appearances in gardens, beginning with the garden of the Hôtel des Trois Couronnes, are suggestive of her Edenic innocence and naturalness. (The Edenic element is highlighted by Mrs. Costello's charge that "[s]he goes on from day to day, from hour to hour, as they did in the Golden Age" [41]). The whole movement of the story may be said to be epitomized by the movement from the garden to the graveyard, a gradual revelation of the sad truth experience brings home to innocence, that death, too, is present in Arcadia. The use of time of day and of season also have symbolic resonance. We not only meet Daisy, the flower, in the garden, but we do so in the morning; when we see her last, just before the flower will close up in death, it is at night in the Colosseum. When we first meet her in Vevey, moreover, it is in the summer; when the scene shifts to Rome, it is winter, "towards the end of January" (24). It is not hard to see that the shift from garden, morning, and summer, to graveyard, night, and winter has the elemental quality of a mythic archetype, and that this whole movement is deepened in its significance by the implications we have already discussed in the names Daisy and Winterbourne.

There are two other points I want to touch on briefly before moving on in the next chapter to a discussion of the sexual politics of *Daisy Miller*. First, there may be some symbolic suggestion in James's having set the story "two or three years ago" (4), for the reader of the original magazine version of 1878 or of the first authorized book version of 1879 might have been expected to place the tale in 1876, the year of the centennial of the American Revolution, another indirect way of emphasizing Daisy's national characteristics, her American love of liberty and independence.[70] Second, I want to repeat a suggestion I made earlier, that while on the realistic level Daisy dies from malaria, symbolically she is stricken down when Winterbourne cuts her. In the revision, incidentally, James emphasizes this by changing her exclamation "he cuts me!" (46) to "he cuts me dead!"[71] To be sure, malaria was pervasive in Rome in Daisy's time and afterwards. The nineteenth-century guidebooks generally devote some prominent preliminary pages to guarding one's health in Rome, but they give curiously contradictory advice. The prefatory material to Baedeker's *Central Italy* warns that "[t]he visitor should be careful not to drive in an open carriage after dark, or to sit in the evening in such malarial places as the Colosseum," but the same volume advises some 250 pages later that "The Colosseum is profoundly impressive by MOONLIGHT. . . . The traveller should avail himself of a fine moonlight night for the purpose."[72] Daisy's death is certainly attributable to malaria, the Roman fever of the guidebooks, but her defenses were undoubtedly lowered by the psychic wound Winterbourne dealt her, and that two-pronged diagnosis of her malady is thoroughly consistent with what I described at the outset of this chapter as James's masterful use of elements that operate at one and the same time realistically and symbolically to forge the enduring myth of *Daisy Miller*.

6

SEXUAL POLITICS AND SOCIAL CLASS

William Butler Yeats once said that the only things worth writing about are sex and death. *Daisy Miller* treats both these topics, foregrounding the first and climaxing with the second. Much of *Daisy Miller* is concerned with sexual politics—with the different ways of treating young unmarried women in America and Europe, with the unequal status of men and women in the second half of the nineteenth century, and with the ways in which networks of social power are governed according to such differentiation. Although, as Leon Edel remarks, "the manners it portrays are outmoded," the underlying issues of human relations remain pressing for us today: the problems of social and economic power inequitably distributed between the sexes, of gender stereotyping, of self-involvement and narcissism that blind individuals to the feelings and needs of others, and of conflict between individual values and desires and the pressure for conformity to group codes.[73]

To understand the reasons that Daisy puzzles Winterbourne and outrages the community of expatriate American matrons in Rome, one must have some notion of the relations that obtained between the sexes in middle and upper class society in the nineteenth century. Some aspects of the conduct expected of young women can readily be inferred from the story itself. Winterbourne is surprised and excited by the freedom with which he finds he is able to approach Daisy Miller on first making her acquaintance because "[i]n Geneva . . . a young man was not at liberty to speak to a young unmarried lady except under certain rarely-occurring conditions" (6). Winterbourne is shocked, as we have noticed in the last chapter, by the contrast between Mrs. Miller's willingness to let Daisy go with him alone to Chillon and the protective vigilance of the "matrons who massed themselves in the forefront of social intercourse" in Geneva (19). Later, in Rome, Daisy makes a scandal of herself by being constantly in Giovanelli's company and by going about with him unchaperoned to the Pincio, St. Peter's, the art gallery of the Doria Palace, and so on. Most readers today, even if they have not studied the culture of the nineteenth century, will recognize that Daisy is violating the European requirement that young unmarried women be constantly under the surveillance of chaperones.

One of the central international contrasts in *Daisy Miller* arises from Daisy's unwitting violation of the system of chaperonage, which operated strictly in England and on the Continent but which, except in some very small social circles that imitated European manners (for example, Mrs. Costello's "minutely hierarchical" New York society [13]), was not followed in the United States. A recent study of the lives of women in Victorian America notes that, in contrast to Europe, "[h]ere, unchaperoned social activity was the norm."[74] This observation is confirmed by the testimony of no less authoritative a contemporary observer of American manners and mores than John Hay (some years later Theodore Roosevelt's secretary of state). Hay observed of Daisy Miller in 1879,

> She is represented, by a chronicler who loves and admires her, as bringing ruin upon herself and a certain degree of discredit upon her country-women, through eccentricities of behavior for which

she cannot justly be held responsible. Her conduct is without blemish, according to the rural American standard, and she knows no other. It is the merest ignorance or affectation, on the part of the anglicized Americans of Boston or New York, to deny this. A few dozens, perhaps a few hundreds, of families in America have accepted the European theory of the necessity of surveillance for young ladies, but it is idle to say it has ever been accepted by the country at large. In every city of the nation young girls of good family, good breeding, and perfect innocence of heart and mind, receive their male acquaintance *en tête-à-tête,* and go to parties and concerts with them, unchaperoned.[75]

Here, by way of contrast, is an account of the European system as practiced in the upper middle class and upper class in England:

The restrictions and conventions of Society were designed to make courtship difficult. "An unmarried woman under thirty could not go anywhere or be in a room even in her own house with an unrelated man unless accompanied by a married gentlewoman or a servant." Young girls could certainly not go unchaperoned to the theatre, dances or restaurants. Few public places were open to women alone, especially those below the critical age of thirty, so that meetings with young men were usually restricted to the home, under careful observation. Daughters paid social calls only in the company of parents or chaperones and while suitable young men might be permitted to call on Sundays, such visits inevitably implied that their intentions were serious. A young girl also had to be careful not to appear to encourage any one man unless she was willing to marry him.

The author of these comments, Pat Jalland, also observes that while "[t]he established aristocracy could perhaps afford to be slightly more relaxed about the rules than the rising middle class," even they "could not expect to ignore Society's rules without risking the sanction of exclusion from desirable drawing-rooms and from sources of alliance and power."[76] In other words, even aristocrats who went against the social code might suffer the kind of ostracism inflicted on Daisy in Rome.

The ideology that underlay the system of chaperonage arose from a sociological, medical, economic, political, religious consensus that women were ordained for the sacred duties of wifehood and motherhood and that nothing should be allowed to deflect or distract them from preparation for and fulfillment of those duties. The ramifications of this ideology in the Victorian world were multifold: women did not have the same legal rights as men (not only with respect to the franchise that was denied women in both England and America until the end of the second decade of the twentieth century, but also with respect to the right to own property and to conduct financial transactions); they were denied access to the professions; and they were denied the expensive educations that prepared their brothers for careers in science, the law, medicine, and other "serious" professions. Women were educated, rather, in matters thought appropriate and not injurious to their wifely and maternal roles: the modern languages, piano playing and singing, needlework, and other such finishing-school attainments. Jalland's footnotes in the passage from which the following quotation is drawn are to various medical and marriage manuals of the period, all written by men, several of them physicians:

> . . . such education as girls received should train them in the noble arts of service and self-sacrifice, transforming devoted daughters into perfect wives and mothers. . . . If women's energies were diverted from reproductive to intellectual ends, the human race would suffer: "During the crisis of puberty . . . there should be a general relaxation from study, which might otherwise too forcibly engross the mind and the energies required by the constitution to work out nature's ends." Writers deplored excessive mental application and intellectual stimulation at the "dawn of womanhood," between the ages of thirteen and sixteen.[77]

The system for regulating the lives of women in every sphere of life, from the biological to the intellectual, was maintained by male authority, principally by fathers, husbands, educators, clergymen, and doctors. Women were under the control of what Virginia Woolf would later call "the patriarchy."

In America women were under somewhat less rigid control than they were in England and Europe, in part because of the comparatively high degree of social mobility in the United States and the concomitant absence here of a rigid class structure. In England, where by and large marriages were no longer arranged by parents but where the institution of marriage was conceived of as a means of maintaining and furthering economic and social interests, rigid social controls such as those embodied in the chaperonage system were required to ensure that young people nominally free to choose their own mates would not find themselves in potential courtship situations with anyone who would be considered unsuitable in class or financial status. Chaperonage, moreover, also expressed Victorian anxieties about sex and sexuality; the Victorians sought to regulate the bestiality they feared stirred beneath the surface of polished manners and elaborate social rituals. As one aristocratic woman wrote in a memoir of Victorian society, "It was supposed that most men were not 'virtuous,' that is, nearly all would be capable of accosting and annoying—or worse—any unaccompanied young woman whom they met."[78] The author of this comment writes movingly, as do many other women of her time and class, of the unutterable frustration and boredom of the imprisonment that strict adherence to chaperonage meant, of long afternoons spent staring out windows wishing to go for a walk and of being unable to do so because there was no suitable chaperone available. The Victorians' fear of lapses in virtue, moreover, included women as well as men, for it was also supposed that many young women, exposed to carnal temptation, would have no powers of resistance.

Despite the less rigid social system in America, including the general absence of chaperonage for young women, many aspects of the Victorian sexual ideology I have just outlined were shared on both sides of the Atlantic. In America, too, women were to be dedicated to the sacred duties of wifehood and motherhood; they would keep the tabernacle of the home while men waged the battle for the almighty dollar in the marketplace. We need look no farther than the James family itself to see that even in an unusually talented and unconventional American family there was no outlet for the energies and gifts of a daughter who did not wish to dedicate herself to the domestic service of wifehood: the tragedy of Alice James (see n. 7) includes many of the same elements of frustration with a circumscribed sphere of expectations and opportunities that would be powerfully voiced by Woolf in *A Room of One's Own* (1929) and *Three Guineas* (1938). In *Daisy Miller,* moreover, we see that Mrs. Miller and Daisy are free to enjoy the leisure of European travel, leisure underwritten by the "substantial Mr. Miller in that mysterious land of dollars" (41). The leisure and conspicuous consumption of the Miller women, who travel while Mr. Miller labors in his "big business" back in Schenectady (8), are thoroughly consistent with the economics and sociology of Victorian gender differentiation on both sides of the Atlantic.

Frederick Winterbourne, it must be said, is something of an anomaly, first in being an American who does not live in America, and second in being an American male who is "not in business" (23). From the vantage point of nineteenth-century American culture, there is something slightly effete in Winterbourne's lack of occupation. His unmasculine detachment from "business" goes hand in hand with his being very much a habitué of a society of women, one ruled by matrons such as his aunt and Mrs. Costello, who act as self-appointed arbiters of the patriarchal social code. On the other hand, Winterbourne enjoys the masculine prerogatives of that code, one that dictated, for example, that whereas young women were to be mentally virginal and physically chaste until marriage, young men could "sow their wild oats," and that whereas young women were to have their social contacts confined to "good" society, young men were free to go slumming socially—or, as Mrs. Costello puts it, making explicit the sexual double standard, "of course a man may know every one. Men are welcome to the privilege!" (25).

I think we are safe in assuming that, were Winterbourne ever to lead a young woman to the bridal chamber, she would not be in the hands of an inexperienced lover: "When his friends spoke of him, they usually said that he was at Geneva, 'studying.' . . . when certain persons spoke of him they affirmed that the reason of his spending so much time at Geneva was that he was extremely devoted to a lady who lived there—a foreign lady—a person older than himself" (4). Some readers have treated this information as ambiguous, suggesting that James does not want us to know for sure whether or not Winterbourne does indeed have a lover in Geneva. I myself find the evidence that he does so quite clear. The quotation marks around the word *studying* in the sentence just quoted strongly suggest that this is the case, and we should note that those coy, suggestive (and I should almost say "winking") quotation marks are repeated in the last sentence of the story: "Nevertheless, he went back to live at Geneva, whence there continue to come the most contradictory reports of his motives of sojourn: a report that he is 'studying' hard—an intimation that he is much interested in a very clever foreign lady" (50). When Daisy guesses that there is a woman in Geneva to whom Winterbourne wishes to hurry back from Vevey, moreover, the narrator's summary of Winterbourne's thoughts would seem to imply a confirmation of the mistress's existence, for Winterbourne wonders, "How did Miss Daisy Miller know that there was a charmer in Geneva?" and he is amazed "at the rapidity of her induction" (24). I would add that the relation that innocent Daisy infers between Winterbourne and the "mysterious charmer" (23–24) would not have, in her mind, any active sexual component, though the reader is surely meant to suppose that there is one. When Mrs.

Costello says to her nephew, with prophetic irony, "You have lived too long out of the country, You will be sure to make some great mistake. You are too innocent," Winterbourne replies, "My dear aunt, I am not so innocent," and his gesture as he does so, "smiling and curling his moustache," is the act of a sexually experienced man of the world: when one smiles and curls one's moustache while saying that one is "not so innocent," a great deal is being said that does not need spelling out (14–15).

Not only is Winterbourne sexually experienced, but also, from the first, he regards women as sexual objects and regards them not as individuals but as members of a class. James's narrator suggests the first point, that Winterbourne regards women as things, when he follows his description of the "flitting hither and thither of 'stylish' young girls" at Vevey (3) with the introductory description of Winterbourne's "looking about him, rather idly, at some of the graceful *objects* I have mentioned" (4; italics added). (James uses "objects" in the same way, incidentally, when he has the villain of *The Portrait of a Lady*, Gilbert Osmond, think about Isabel Archer as a "figure in his collection of choice objects."[79] James probably derived Osmond's sinister wording from the duke in Robert Browning's "My Last Duchess," who assures the emissary of a count that "his fair daughter's self, as I avowed / At starting, is my object.") Winterbourne himself illustrates the second point, that he does not see women as individuals, when he exclaims to himself, on first seeing Daisy, "How pretty they are!" (6)—not "How pretty she is!" which would have distinguished Daisy as a particular person and not as a representative of a type. As he overcomes his initial embarrassment about the informality and the possible impropriety with which his acquaintance with Daisy begins, Winterbourne dwells at greater length on her beauty, and we are told that "[h]e had a great relish for feminine beauty; he was addicted to observing it and analysing it" (7). His thoughts, meanwhile, turn very quickly to his attempts to classify her, to place her in a category that is familiar to him: "Never . . . had he encountered a young American girl of so pronounced a type as this. . . . He had known, here in Europe, two or three women—persons older than Miss Daisy Miller, and provided, for respectability's sake, with husbands—who were great coquettes—dangerous, terrible women, with whom one's relations were liable to take a serious turn. But this young girl was not a coquette in that sense; she was very unsophisticated; she was only a pretty American flirt. Winterbourne was almost grateful for having found the formula that applied to Miss Daisy Miller" (10).

Winterbourne's efforts to pigeonhole Daisy, to classify her definitively, once and for all, are comically attenuated throughout almost the whole story. She appears innocent, but her behavior so exceeds conventional European expectations of young women that he cannot decide if she is a "nice" girl or one who is given to "lawless passions" (32). Against the imputations of Mrs. Costello and Mrs. Walker, he gallantly defends Daisy, telling his aunt that Daisy and her mother "are very ignorant, very innocent only," that they are "not bad" (25), and telling Mrs. Walker that "The poor girl's only fault . . . is that she is very uncultivated" (35). Still, Winterbourne's character lacks a good deal in self-trust and integrity. The attacks of the matrons on Daisy's virtue erode his faith in Daisy, preparing him for that ultimate moment of "relief" in the Colosseum when he feels that "the riddle had become easy to read" and decides that Daisy is "a young lady whom a gentleman need no longer be at pains to respect" (46). Of course, he is wrong, as he learns at Daisy's funeral, and, as I have suggested, the chilly treatment that he gives Daisy after coming to his mistaken conclusion contributes in some way to her death.

Lest we judge Winterbourne too harshly, we should remember that he is considerably more open-minded about the possibility of Daisy's being innocent than the authoritative matrons of the expatriate community. We might be inclined to condemn him for a Prufrock-like inability to make up his mind, but the reader would do well to restrain that temptation and to take to heart Richard Hocks's compelling observation that "as long as Winterbourne remained truly puzzled by the question of Daisy's sexual innocence he was potentially worthy of her and worthy of our sympathetic engagement with him as narrative 'center.'"[80] Indeed, there are other points on which we might judge Winterbourne even more harshly, and yet I would suggest that in these matters too Winterbourne is as much a victim of Victorian sexual ideology as Daisy. For example, we might note that he is constantly torn between his desire that Daisy be "good," expressed in his defense of her innocence in the face of attacks by others, and his barely repressed desire that she be "bad," which comes out in his fantasies about her during the excursion to Chillon, when he feels that he is off on "an escapade—an adventure" (22), "could have believed that he was going to elope with her" (21), and feels disappointed that she wants to go on the steamer since he would have preferred the intimacy of a carriage ride. Would it not be fair to Winterbourne to say that this vacillation between defenses of Daisy's honor, on the one hand, and fantasies of illicit sexual adventure with her, on the other, is the result of his Victorian, Europeanized upbringing, which requires the first behavior as an element in protective, masculine gallantry and which makes the second, fantasized behavior almost inevitable by allowing no approved means for the open expression of male sexual desire where "nice girls" are concerned? As Lauren Cowdery suggests, "Rather than blaming Winterbourne for devising this view of women all by himself, we should see it for what it is—an unthinking reflection of the conventional system of stereotypes—and appreciate the way James begins to call that system into question. . . . James's accomplishment is to induce in his readers a revulsion against a way of viewing women which is related to the way polite society 'cages' Julia Bride [the title character of a later James story]. A character compounded of social conditioning, ignorance of self, and the worried desire to be fair is a fit representative of a harmful society, more so than the dowagers untroubled by self-doubt."[81]

James wants us to see that the attempt to find "the formula" for another human being is injurious, an act of violence and of violation of the unique individuality of the other. At the same time, Winterbourne's first formula for Daisy, that she is "a pretty American flirt" (10), is accurate as far as it goes, though of course it is woefully incomplete. At Mrs. Walker's soirée Winterbourne says to Daisy, "I'm afraid your habits are those of a flirt." "Of course they are," Daisy replies. "I'm a fearful, frightful flirt! Did you ever hear of a nice girl that was not?" (38). It is important to understand that there is no violation of consistency for Daisy to be at one and the same time an innocent and a flirt. Flirting, after all, is a species of sexual banter or teasing. It is primarily verbal, and it ceases to be flirtation if it proceeds beyond play, which, in Daisy's case, it never does. Edward Wagenknecht has recently reminded us that "[a]s used in this tale [*Daisy Miller*], 'flirt' is only mildly pejorative."[82] I would suggest, however, that "flirt" need not be even mildly pejorative. Daisy's flirtatious behavior and her question—"Did you ever hear of a nice girl that was not" a flirt?—are simply in accord with American courtship rituals. "Flirting," observes the author of a recent book subtitled *An Intimate View of the Lives of Women in Victorian America*, "was socially acceptable as a way for a young woman to reveal her social grace and her availability to prospective suitors," and he quotes *Godey's Lady's Book and Magazine* (July 1860): "Flirting is to marriage what free trade is to commerce. By it the value of a woman is exhibited, tested, her capacities known, her temper displayed, and the opportunity offered of judging what sort of a wife she may probably become."[83] Even Winterbourne seems to acknowledge the customary nature of flirtation in America when he tells Daisy, "Flirting is a purely American custom; it doesn't exist here" (38).

Daisy is largely ignorant of her affronts to the social code. In Vevey there is no hint whatsoever that she knows how surprising Winterbourne finds her behavior and that of her mother. In Rome she appears to have plunged with gay abandon at first into the pleasures of being "surrounded by a half-dozen wonderful moustaches" (25). Soon enough, however, she is apprised by Mrs. Walker and Winterbourne, and then by her systematic exclusion from American society in Rome, of the way her behavior is damaging her reputation and creating a scandal. We recall James's remark to Mrs. Linton that though the word *defiant* is used in the tale it was not intended in any "large sense" but merely to describe "the state of her poor little heart" (see n. 30). James, however, seems not to have consulted his own text closely in framing his letter to Mrs. Linton, for Winterbourne, whether correctly or not, at times attributes a defiant *consciousness* to Daisy Miller: "He said to himself that she was too light and childish, too uncultivated and unreasoning, too provincial, to have reflected upon her ostracism or even to have perceived it. Then at other moments he believed that she carried about in her elegant and irresponsible little organism a defiant, passionate, perfectly observant consciousness of the impression she produced" (43). Although we need to be careful not to inflate Daisy's conscious defiance and criticism of the society that ostracizes her too much beyond the innocence that Henry James attributes to her, there is, I would suggest, strong evidence that she is significantly more critically aware than his letter to Mrs. Linton allows.

If Daisy is at first unaware that her constantly being with Giovanelli, her "dancing all the evening with the same partners" (35), and her walking on the Pincio with Winterbourne and Giovanelli grievously offend the taboos already surveyed in this chapter, she is nevertheless quite pointed at times in her responses to those who seek to disabuse her of her social ignorance. Her idea that having Winterbourne with her will make it all right for her to walk with Giovanelli looks forward to a scene in James's *The Portrait of a Lady,* when the American girl Isabel Archer is told by her aunt that she cannot sit up at night in the aunt's house alone with two young men, one of whom is her cousin. "You are not—you are not at Albany, my dear," says Isabel's aunt. "I wish I were," Isabel replies, and, she goes on to say, "I always want to know the things one shouldn't do." "So as to do them?" asks the aunt. "So as to choose," says Isabel, reserving to herself the same right, it seems to me, that Daisy exercises on the Pincio.[84]

Just before she recruits Winterbourne to come with her, Daisy responds to Mrs. Walker's appeal—"My dear young friend . . . don't walk off to the Pincio at this hour to meet a beautiful Italian"—with an exclamatory "Gracious me! . . . I don't want to do anything improper" (29). But when Mrs. Walker tries to command Daisy to abandon the young men on their walk and to join her, for the sake of making a respectable appearance, in her carriage, Daisy replies with spirit that behavior such as hers "ought to be" the custom, that "I am more than five years old," and that, in regard to Mrs. Walker's statement that Daisy is "old enough . . . to be talked about," "I don't think I want to know what you mean. . . . I don't think I should like it" (33–34). When Winterbourne utters his concurrence with Mrs. Walker, Daisy becomes, I would say, most consciously defiant, declaring, "I never heard anything so stiff! If this is improper, Mrs. Walker, . . . then I am all improper, and you must give me up" (34). Daisy makes clear, moreover, that she is choosing, as Isabel Archer would wish to do, when she tells Winterbourne three days later that she defied Mrs. Walker in order to spare Giovanelli's feelings: "But did you ever hear anything so cool as Mrs. Walker's wanting me to get into her carriage and drop poor Mr. Giovanelli; and under the pretext that it was proper? People have different ideas! It would have been most unkind; he had been talking about that walk for ten days" (38).

People do have different ideas. For Daisy, the greater impropriety is not to *appear* "a very reckless girl" (34) by walking with Giovanelli but to *be* unkind to her friend by disappointing and abandoning him. Daisy later implies that there is a moral imperative to be kind that should supersede adherence to the social code when she tells Winterbourne, apropos of Mrs. Walker's having cut her and of Winterbourne's warning that others "will give you the cold shoulder," "I shouldn't think you would let people be so unkind!" (45). Daisy most certainly offers a critique of the reigning sexual ideology when she answers Winterbourne's charge that flirting is not understood "in young unmarried women" with the riposte, "It seems to me much more proper in young unmarried women than in old married ones" (38), which should remind us of Winterbourne's experience of "dangerous, terrible women" who were "provided, for respectability's sake, with husbands" (10). Most impressively, Daisy intuits that society is much more concerned with appearances than with actuality, is concerned above all with the look of respectability and of innocence. "They are only pretending to be shocked," she tells Winterbourne. "They don't give a straw what I do" (44): what is implicit in this speech is her insight that what concerns the Mrs. Walkers of the world is not what she does but what she *appears* to do.

I infer from this evidence that the text of the tale endows Daisy with a moral consciousness and with some conscious defiance of the code of behavior that condemned her, regardless of her creator's statement otherwise—after the fact. I believe that, as Richard Hocks suggests, Daisy is drawn in part, like other great James heroines (notably Isabel Archer in *The Portrait of a Lady* and Milly Theale in *The Wings of the Dove*), after James's beloved cousin Minnie Temple, who died, like Daisy, prematurely, and whom James admired especially for her "moral spontaneity," a quality he thought particularly American and that he noted was absent in English young women.[85] Daisy shares something of Minnie's vitality, her courage, and her gallantry, even if she is deficient in other areas in which

Minnie was strong, especially in her barren awareness of culture and utter lack of intellectuality.

And this brings me to the last brief point I want to make before going on to consider the plot and structure of *Daisy Miller*. Daisy's lack of culture is one of several signs—along with, among others, her "familiarity" with servants, her offense against Winterbourne's sense of caste when she suggests that he be Randolph's tutor (23), and the vulgarity of her mother's "pathological gossip" (27)—that Daisy's breeding is not, even by American standards, good.[86] John Hay says as much in his "Contributor's Club" comments, following his observation that American "girls of good breeding, good family" regularly go about unchaperoned with the remark, "Of course, I do not mean that Daisy Miller belongs to that category; her astonishing mother at once designates her as pertaining to one distinctly inferior" (see n. 75). It must be said that the efforts of Mrs. Walker to inculcate Daisy with the standards of proper behavior can only be, from the point of view of a Mrs. Costello, at best an act of condescension and of charity. Mrs. Costello's revulsion from Daisy is a matter of class exclusivity even before Daisy commits any of her supposed outrages to decency. Daisy is very wealthy, "dresses in perfection" as Mrs. Costello acknowledges (13), and is able to afford the poshest resorts, such as the Hôtel de Trois Couronnes, but she is "common," she "has an intimacy with her mamma's courier" (14), and for such offenses Mrs. Costello would have declined to meet her even if Daisy's behavior had not given her any other excuses for doing so. The Millers are nouveau riche. They do not have the class, the sophistication, or the cultural attainments of the older, exclusive families of New York and Boston who would constitute good society for Winterbourne's "exclusive" aunt (16). Class prejudice as well as indignation over the American girl's violations of the social code contribute to the ostracism of Daisy Miller.

7

PLOT AND STRUCTURE

Henry James advocated polished, balanced form in fiction. He developed a masterful sense of aesthetic form, of tight artistic control, qualities that were virtually unknown before him in fiction in English and that had only a few pioneers in Continental novelists, particularly Flaubert and Turgenev. In the prefaces he wrote for the late New York Edition of his work he put forward an unprecedented, lucid, critically sophisticated handbook, as it were, of fiction considered as an art and not merely as a form of popular entertainment. Many of James's ideas, most prominently his theories on point of view, were so persuasively formulated later by various commentators that James appears to have governed the terms of critical discourse on the art of fiction throughout most of the twentieth century.[87] I would add that James's ideas were often tentative and his practice was flexible, not constrained by any artistic dogma, his own or anyone else's. In erecting James's critical essays into a doctrine, his followers have in some degree unwittingly betrayed the legacy of an artist who never let himself become subservient to any doctrine, who, as T. S. Eliot put the matter in one of his several tributes to James, "had a mind so fine that no idea could violate it"—that is, no idea could violate the integrity with which James respected the complexity and ambiguity of any matter to which he turned his attention.[88]

James's integrity, his insistence on looking all round an issue or a situation (as opposed to seeing it from just one side), and his dedication to economical, well-proportioned artistic form are strongly in evidence throughout *Daisy Miller*. We can see how he advances these concerns throughout the plot and overall structure of the story. For example, if we consider the second paragraph to be the real opening of the story—considering the first paragraph, before the viewpoint becomes predominantly Winterbourne's, to be a sort of prologue—then we can appreciate the roundness James gives the story by ending it with a sentence that closely echoes the language at the start about Winterbourne's sojourn in Geneva being due to his "studying" or to his devotion to a "foreign lady" (4, 50). We notice also that Winterbourne's conversations with Mrs. Costello occur at fairly regular intervals, the last ironically echoing the first in his admission that "You were right in that remark that you made last summer. I was booked to make a mistake. I have lived too long in foreign parts" (50).

In terms of large structure, *Daisy Miller* is divided into four sections of approximately equal length, with a symmetrical division between the two summer chapters in Vevey and the two winter chapters in Rome (these two halves correspond to the two parts of the original serialization in *Cornhill Magazine*). Thus important incidents in each half of the story have balancing counterparts in the other half: for instance, Winterbourne's socially daring conversations with unchaperoned Daisy in the garden of the Hôtel des Trois Couronnes are balanced by Giovanelli's scandal-provoking outings with Daisy in the Pincian Gardens and amid the "flowering desolation" of the Palatine Hill (43); Mrs. Costello's refusal to meet Daisy in Vevey is balanced by Mrs. Walker's cutting her at the soirée and by Daisy's general exclusion from "good society" in Rome. Winterbourne's excursion with Daisy to the Castle of Chillon, which seems to him so unusual that it constitutes "an escapade—an adventure" (22), is balanced by a parallel incident, Giovanelli's perilous (not to say lethal) escorting of Daisy to the moonlit Colosseum. James's balancing of such key incidents can have important thematic implications. The Colosseum-Chillon balance, for instance, retrospectively casts Winterbourne in the same role as Giovanelli, which tends to discredit Winterbourne. Though he rebukes Giovanelli for not protecting Daisy as a gentleman should have done, we may recall, as we notice the parallel episodes, that Winterbourne not only engaged in fantasies of the illicit during the Chillon excursion but also actually bribed the custodian there to make sure that he and Daisy were alone during their time in the castle.

An element of James's construction of the story related to his duplication of episodes is his masterful foreshadowing, which we have already observed in the first paragraph of the story. I want here simply to lay to rest the idea that Daisy's death is inadequately prepared for—an idea wrongly advanced, it seems to me, in one of the better essays on *Daisy Miller,* Carol Ohmann's, which argues that the denouement is at best crudely foreshadowed by a couple of sentences in the second half of the story (see n. 41). Even before Mrs. Miller warns Daisy that if she walks on the Pincio with Giovanelli "You'll get the fever as sure as you live" and that "Your friend won't keep you from getting the fever" (29), and before Daisy herself tells Winterbourne, "We are going to stay [in Rome] all winter—if we don't die of the fever; and I guess we'll stay then" (30), there is a subtly premonitory bit of dialogue between Daisy and Winterbourne on the steamer to Chillon:

> "What on *earth* are you so grave about," she suddenly demanded, fixing her agreeable eyes upon Winterbourne's.
> "Am I grave?" he asked. "I had an idea I was grinning from ear to ear."
> "You look as if you were taking me to a funeral." (22)

The repetition of the word *grave* in combination with the word *funeral* makes the first word into a Shakespearean pun, as in the dying Mercutio's statement "Ask for me tomorrow, and you shall find me a grave man" (*Romeo and Juliet* 3.1.95–96). The image of Winterbourne grinning "from ear to ear"—though it is only his idea of himself, not the reality ("If that's a grin, your ears are very near together," Daisy teases)—suggests a skull, a death's-head, which would appear to grin from ear to ear (like the skull of Yorick in *Hamlet,* which has "[n]ot one [gibe, a jest or song] now to mock your own grinning" [5.1.179–80]). The suggested skull, moreover, is not just a memento mori but also more precisely, as we reread, a forecast that the story will end with a burial and that the grave will be Daisy's ("Am I grave?" "You look as if you were taking me to a funeral").[89]

The light, rapid strokes with which James develops *Daisy Miller* are economically concentrated in just a few well-chosen occasions. Chapter 1 consists of a single scene, the first encounter, on a June morning, between Daisy and Winterbourne in the hotel garden. Chapter 2 divides into three scenes, first Winterbourne's conversation with his aunt on the afternoon of the same day, then his talk with Daisy that evening, again in the garden, and, finally, two days later, the trip to Chillon, with a brief coda, a five-line conversation between Winterbourne and Mrs. Costello. Chapter 3 has a brief, introductory scene between Winterbourne and Mrs. Costello, but it is mostly devoted to a sustained dramatic action that covers three locales (the drawing room, the Pincio, and the carriage) and that comprises Winterbourne's meeting of Daisy, Mrs. Miller, and Randolph in Mrs. Walker's drawing room, the conversation there that culminates in the dispute about Daisy's imminent walk on the Pincio with Giovanelli, and then the walk itself, featuring a dramatic climax in Daisy's refusal to join Mrs. Walker in her carriage, and a second, subsidiary climax in Winterbourne's leaving the carriage after he has climbed in for a colloquy with Mrs. Walker. Chapter 4, finally, contains a series of dramatic scenes: the soirée at which Mrs. Walker cuts Daisy; the scene in which Winterbourne and his aunt discuss Daisy Miller in St. Peter's, where they have noticed Daisy and Giovanelli together; the very brief dialogue between Winterbourne and an unnamed friend who tells him about having seen Daisy and Giovanelli together in the Doria Palace; a brief dialogue between Winterbourne and Mrs. Miller when Winterbourne calls at the Millers' hotel; the scene on the Palatine Hill when Daisy teases Winterbourne about whether she and Giovanelli are engaged; the climactic scene in the Colosseum; Daisy's funeral; and the final dialogue between Winterbourne and his aunt. Each episode is more crowded with incidents than the preceding one, creating a sense of rising, accelerating action, of quickening pace and heightening intensity.

CHAPTER 1: "SHE'S AN AMERICAN GIRL"

Let us look at the story chapter by chapter, observing some of the principal developments in each, concentrating particularly on points that have not been covered in the preceding discussions. As Leon Edel has emphasized, a major theme of *Daisy Miller* is "the total abdication, by the mass of American parents, of all authority over their children."[90] This theme, developed throughout the story, is powerfully introduced in the first chapter in Randolph's ungoverned and ungovernable behavior, beginning with his first, rude speech to Winterbourne—"Will you give me a lump of sugar?" (4)—and including Daisy's information to Winterbourne that Randolph does not have a tutor because the child has willfully opposed the idea ("He said he wouldn't have lessons when he was in the cars" [8]) and that Randolph's lack of interest in the sights of Europe has largely confined the Miller party to their hotels ("He says he don't care much about old castles. He's only nine. He wants to stay at the hotel. Mother's afraid to leave him alone, and the courier won't stay with him; so we haven't been to many places" [11]). The same theme of a failure of parental supervision is implicit in Winterbourne's amazement at the situation he finds himself in with Daisy, conversing with a young woman who seems blandly to take unchaperoned encounters with young men as a matter of course and who titillates Winterbourne's imagination at the end of the chapter by proposing that the two of them go alone to Chillon:

> "Eugenio's our courier. He doesn't like to stay with Randolph; he's the most fastidious man I ever saw. . . . I guess he'll stay at home with Randolph if mother does, and then we can go to the castle."
> Winterbourne reflected for an instant as lucidly as possible— "we" could only mean Miss Miller and himself. This programme seemed almost too agreeable for credence; he felt as if he ought to kiss the young lady's hand. Possibly he would have done so—and quite spoiled the project; but at this moment another person— presumably Eugenio—appeared. (11–12)

The narrator's interpolation that had Winterbourne kissed Daisy he would have "quite spoiled the project" suggests, incidentally, that whereas Winterbourne's sexual feeling for Daisy is already aroused by the prospect of an excursion that would violate the taboos by which he lives, Daisy is quite ignorant of how her behavior appears to him, is innocent of the least blush of the illicit in her proposal, and would have been shocked into retreat, despite the informality of her own manners, had Winterbourne been so forward as to kiss her hand. Despite her unsupervised state, moreover, Daisy does show some social circumspection in questioning Winterbourne on his bona fides—"And you are staying at this hotel? . . . And you are really an American?" (12)—whereupon Winterbourne makes a promise he will not be able to keep, to introduce Daisy to his aunt in order, as he tells Mrs. Costello in the next chapter, "to guarantee my respectability" (14).

Daisy's question about whether Winterbourne is really an American repeats an earlier query: "She asked him if he was a 'real American'; she wouldn't have taken him for one; he seemed more like a German" (7).[91] Her puzzlement about Winterbourne mirrors his about her. In fact, perhaps the central accomplishment of the first chapter is to introduce us to the culturally conditioned misunderstandings these two young people have of each other, and Daisy's thought that Winterbourne might be German is one of the early clues that he is as much a mystery to her as she is to him. Of course, we know how puzzled Winterbourne is because he is the point-of-view character ("Poor Winterbourne was amused, perplexed, and decidedly charmed" [10]); Daisy's puzzlement can only be inferred from her words and actions. Evidently she has never encountered in a "real American" the reserve in manners and formality in speech that Winterbourne exhibits.

Daisy's national character is proclaimed loudly by Randolph when he announces his sister's approach: "'Here comes my sister!' cried the child, in a moment. 'She's an American girl'" (5). Daisy's American quality is conveyed not only in negative terms (e.g., that she is ignorant of European manners) but also in positive ones (e.g., that her "glance was perfectly direct and unshrinking," not "immodest," but "singularly honest and fresh" [7]). Winterbourne is nearly as shocked by her treating him as an old friend as he is by her lack of embarrassment at not being formally introduced and protectively chaperoned. "She talked to Winterbourne as if she had known him a long time" (9), and she presumes upon their brief acquaintance with what can only have seemed to him an imposition: "I wish *you* would stay with him [Randolph]" she says to Winterbourne (11). He is nevertheless greatly impressed with her beauty, from her first appearance ("Winterbourne . . . saw a beautiful young lady advancing" [5]) to the end of the chapter ("Winterbourne . . . looking after her . . . said to himself that she had the *tournure* of a princess" [12]).

One other important aspect of Daisy is introduced in chapter 1: intellectually and culturally, she is impoverished. Of this element of Daisy's makeup, Richard Hocks observes, "She 'chatters' in a way that . . . sometimes resembles more the sound of a scattergun than the verbalization of real thought. That she is only one step removed from her mother is at times painfully obvious. And the fact that the two of them share in central and southern Europe only the topics of brother Randolph and Schenectady's Dr. Davis is wincing."[92] Daisy tells Winterbourne of her love of society ("'I have always had,' she said, 'a great deal of gentlemen's society'"[10]), but her experience of Europe, of the riches of art and civilization that made the Continent a vast, living museum for earnest American travelers (like the Reverend Babcock in James's earlier novel *The American*), is that it is "nothing but hotels" (9). What, indeed, could be more insipid—more air-headed, we might say today—than her declaring to Winterbourne "that Europe was perfectly sweet"? James might have said of her, as he said years later of Edith Wharton's husband, that she is "cerebrally compromised." The theme of Daisy's intellectual vapidity, moreover, is sustained throughout the story, when, for instance, Winterbourne's spiel about Bonivard at Chillon goes "into one ear and out of the other" (23) and when she tells Winterbourne that she had been afraid that Rome would be "awfully poky," that it would just be "going round all the time with one of those dreadful old men that explain about the pictures and things," but that "we only had about a week of that, and now I'm enjoying myself" (30). Compare Daisy's experience of Rome to Henry James's own first response to the Eternal City, as reported in a letter to his brother William (30 October 1869):

> At last—for the first time—I live! It beats everything: it leaves the Rome of your fancy—your education—nowhere. It makes Venice—Florence—Oxford—London—seem like little cities of pasteboard. I went reeling and moaning thro' the streets in a fever of

enjoyment. In the course of four or five hours I traversed almost the whole of Rome and got a glimpse of everything—the Forum, the Coliseum (stupendissimo!), the Pantheon, the Capitol, St. Peter's, the Column of Trajan, the Castle of St. Angelo—all the Piazzas and ruins and monuments. The effect is something indescribable. For the first time I know what the picturesque is. . . . Even if I should leave Rome tonight, I should feel that I have caught the keynote of its operation on the senses. I have looked along the grassy vista of the Appian Way and seen the topmost stone-work of the Coliseum sitting shrouded in the light of heaven, like the edge of an Alpine chain. I've trod the Forum and I have scaled the Capitol. I've seen the Tiber hurrying along, as swift and dirty as history![93]

James was to some extent showing off his sensibility in letters he knew would be read by a circle beyond his family—two months later he wrote to William, "I am extremely glad you like my letters—and terrifically agitated by the thought that Emerson likes them"—but even so the contrast between his enthusiastic immersion in the intoxicating, historical grandeur of Rome and Daisy's flat indifference is, to borrow Hocks's term, wincing.[94]

CHAPTER 2: "THAT'S ALL I WANT—A LITTLE FUSS!"

Chapter 2 extends all of the threads woven into chapter 1 and introduces a few new ones. The chapter begins and ends with intimations of the way in which Winterbourne waltzes attendance on women. At the outset we learn of how assiduous he is to please his aunt, for "[h]e had imbibed at Geneva the idea that one must always be attentive to his aunt," and this imperative is no doubt strengthened by Mrs. Costello's "fortune" and Winterbourne's having already established with her the reputation of being "more attentive than those who, as she said, were nearer to her" (13). Inheritance is never far from the minds of the Victorian middle class; death, like marriage, was an event particularly graced in the Victorian mind with economic opportunity. At the end of the chapter, as I noted in my comments on sexual politics, Winterbourne is amazed by the rapidity with which Daisy guesses that what is calling him back to Geneva is another woman. In view of these indications of his subservience to women, we are not surprised to find that, after the scene on the Pincio, he heads straight for "the residence of his aunt, Mrs. Costello" (36), that the closing vignette has him once again with his aunt at Vevey, and that the last phrase in the story describes his interest "in a very clever foreign lady" (50). Nor are we surprised that, though he defends Daisy's innocence to Mrs. Costello and Mrs. Walker, he constantly takes counsel with them and comes decisively to their point of view when he mistakenly interprets the encounter in the Colosseum as a revelation of Daisy's disreputability.

The dialogue with Mrs. Costello at the beginning of chapter 2 serves several other purposes. First, it decisively places Daisy in terms of social class, a matter to which we paid some brief attention at the end of the last chapter. Mrs. Costello needs to say no more than "Oh, yes, I have observed them. Seen them—heard them—and kept out of their way." Winterbourne "immediately perceived, from her tone, that Miss Daisy Miller's place in the social scale was low" (13). On the other hand, especially since it comes from someone whom we might aptly term a hostile witness, Mrs. Costello's praise of Daisy's charm and stylishness strongly validates the attractions of the American girl: "She has that charming look they all have. . . . and she dresses in perfection—no, you don't know how well she dresses" (13). Mrs. Costello's fastidious distaste for the Millers' chumminess with servants, expressed in her declaration that "She is a young lady . . . who has an intimacy with her mamma's courier" (13–14), introduces a word, *intimacy,* that, as it recurs later, reverberates with sexual connotations to which Winterbourne is attuned whereas Daisy, as usual, seems innocent of them (e.g., Daisy's saying to Winterbourne, "we are neither of us [she and Giovanelli] flirting; we are too good friends for that; we are very intimate friends" [38]). Another word of Mrs. Costello's that echoes later on is *dreadful*: "What a dreadful girl!" she says of Daisy on learning that the proposal of the excursion to Chillon had come after an acquaintance of only half an hour (14). On the Pincio Mrs. Walker will express her view of Daisy's behavior with the same word: "It's really too dreadful" (32). Although Winterbourne defends Daisy in the face of his aunt's refusal to meet her ("She is completely uncultivated. . . . But . . . she is very nice" [14]), he is characteristically unsure of his ground and eager for Mrs. Costello's insight into the puzzle of Miss Daisy Miller:

> "You really think then," he began, earnestly, and with a desire for trustworthy information—"you really think that—" But he paused again.
> "Think what, sir?" said his aunt.
> "That she is the sort of young lady who expects a man—sooner or later—to carry her off?"
> "I haven't the least idea what such young ladies expect a man to do. But I really think you had better not meddle with little American girls that are uncultivated, as you call them. You have lived too long out of the country. You will be sure to make some great mistake." (14)

Finally, Winterbourne thinks that, since Daisy "exceeded the liberal license allowed" to Mrs. Costello's granddaughters (who he has heard are "tremendous flirts"), "it was probable that anything might be expected of her." This probability makes him "impatient to see her again," an attitude that would seem to confirm the idea that Winterbourne's sexual imagination is titillated by the thought of how far Daisy might go in conventionally unsanctioned behavior (15).

The following long scene in the hotel garden between Daisy and Winterbourne, joined by Mrs. Miller and finally by

Eugenio, contains a number of important developments at which we have already glanced. In Daisy's fluttered, tremorous response to Mrs. Costello's refusal to meet her we get a brief glimpse of her inner life. At the same time Winterbourne's readiness "to sacrifice his aunt conversationally; to admit that she was a proud, rude woman, and to declare that they needn't mind her" is condemned by the narrator as a "perilous mixture of gallantry and impiety" (17). In the discussion of Randolph's refusal to go to bed and in Winterbourne's amazement over Mrs. Miller's lack of protective vigilance in response to Daisy's proposed excursion with him to Chillon, we see a continuation of the theme of the abdication of parental responsibility. The humor of the story is kept up throughout this scene, in, for instance, Daisy's explanation of how she and her mother are "exclusive" ("We don't speak to every one—or they don't speak to us. I suppose it's about the same thing" [16]) and in the cartoonlike, comic caricature of Mrs. Miller, who advances with "a slow and wavering movement," who "hovered vaguely," and who presents "a wandering eye, a very exiguous nose, and a large forehead, decorated with a certain amount of thin, much frizzled hair" (17–18). One notable new element in this incident is Daisy's flirtatious love of teasing, through which it becomes evident that she is at once charmed, puzzled, and irritated by Winterbourne's reserve and formality, an aspect of him that she later formulates negatively, in chapter 3, in what will become her favorite word for him: *stiff*. The whole dialogue about the boat ride exhibits this teasing side of Daisy. She twits Winterbourne with "I'm sure Mr. Winterbourne wants to take me. . . . He's so awfully devoted!" To his romantic offer, "I will row you over to Chillon in the starlight," she teases, "I don't believe it!" She delights in provoking him to characteristic formalities of speech, exulting that "I like a gentleman to be formal" and "I was bound I would make you say something" in response to his elaborate politeness, "If you will do me the honour to accept my arm" (20). But she also delights when he descends to a less formal diction, responding, "It's quite lovely, the way you say that," when he entreats, "Do, then, let me give you a row" (20). In the end, in the face of disapproval from her mother and Eugenio, Daisy declines the boat ride, capping her teasing with the announcement that "I hoped you would make a fuss! . . . That's all I want—a little fuss!" (21).

Daisy resumes her teasing of Winterbourne on the trip to Chillon, submitting him to merciless "*persiflage*" about his presumed "mysterious charmer in Geneva" and at last "telling him she would stop 'teasing' him if he would promise her solemnly to come down to Rome in the winter" (23–24). The counterpart of Winterbourne's barely repressed sexual fantasies about Daisy on this occasion is her much more innocent, more open expression of romantic interest in him that comes out in her suggestion that he join the Miller party as tutor to Randolph, in her being "so agitated by the announcement of his movements," in the acerbity with which she turns her fire on the conjectured rival in Geneva, and in her wish that he come to Rome: "'I don't want you to come for your aunt,' said Daisy. 'I want you to come for me'" (23–24). Finally, the chapter closes with a typical Jamesian roundness, the brief conversation with Mrs. Costello repeating the sniffish disdain with which she declines to be introduced to Daisy in the opening dialogue: "Mrs. Costello sniffed a little at her smelling-bottle. 'And that,' she exclaimed, 'is the young person you wanted me to know!'" (24).

CHAPTER 3: "I AM ALL IMPROPER, AND YOU MUST GIVE ME UP"

With the shift from Vevey to Rome, the story begins to take on a darker tone, beginning with another Mrs. Costello–Winterbourne dialogue. His aunt informs him that in Rome Daisy "rackets about in a way that makes much talk," that the Millers are "hopelessly vulgar"—"very dreadful people," she says, repeating her adjective of the preceding chapter—and that Daisy "has picked up half-a-dozen of the regular Roman fortune-hunters" (25). This last point introduces us to the idea that Daisy, as an American heiress, is a potential victim of less well heeled Europeans who would seek to marry her not for love but for her money—a fate that befalls James's most famous later heroines, Isabel Archer in *The Portrait of a Lady,* Milly Theale in *The Wings of the Dove,* and Maggie Verver in *The Golden Bowl.* Later Mrs. Costello will speculate that Eugenio has played pander for Giovanelli in introducing him to Daisy and that if Giovanelli "succeeds in marrying the young lady, the courier will come in for a magnificent commission" (41). (This hint of collusion between Giovanelli and Eugenio was made by James into a villainous fact in his melodramatic stage version *Daisy Miller: A Comedy in Three Acts* [1882], a version that ends happily with Daisy alive and engaged to Winterbourne. The play, vastly inferior to the story and never produced, will not concern us further.)

After the Winterbourne–Costello dialogue, chapter 3 is devoted to the sustained action beginning in Mrs. Walker's drawing room and continuing through the scene on the Pincio. Daisy continues to express interest in Winterbourne, twice chiding him for not having come to see her immediately upon his arrival in Rome, and also complaining of his departure from Vevey. "My dearest young lady," he replies to the latter charge, "have I come all the way to Rome to encounter your reproaches?" whereupon Daisy, continuing in the delight in Winterbourne's formal speech and in the teasing developed in chapter 2, exclaims, "Just hear him say that! . . . Did you ever hear anything so quaint?" (28). The dramatic highlights of the walk on the Pincio are Daisy's declarations of independence (e.g., "I have never allowed a gentleman to dictate to me, or to interfere with anything I do" [31], "I am more than five years old" [33], "If this is improper, Mrs. Walker, . . . then I am all improper, and you must give me up" [34]) and Winterbourne's refusal of Mrs. Walker's request that he should "cease your relations with Miss Miller," to which he replies, "I'm afraid I can't do that. . . . I like her extremely" (35). In this episode, too, we are introduced to Mr. Giovanelli; despite the Italian's "obsequious" amiability (31), Winterbourne feels "a superior indignation at his own lovely fellow-countrywoman's not knowing the difference between a spurious gentleman and a real one" (32).

Not only does the episode on the Pincio allow Mrs. Walker to make clear the dire social consequences Daisy faces if she continues in her independent carelessness about the mores of the Europeanized American community in Rome, but it also throws Winterbourne once more into his inveterate perplexity about Daisy:

> And then he came back to the question of whether this was in fact a nice girl. Would a nice girl—even allowing for her being a little American flirt—make a rendezvous with a presumably low-lived foreigner? . . . Singular though it may seem, Winterbourne was vexed that the young girl, in joining her *amoroso*, should not appear more impatient of his own company, and he was vexed because of his inclination. It was impossible to regard her as a perfectly well-conducted young lady. . . . It would therefore simplify matters greatly to be able to treat her as the object of one of those sentiments which are called by romancers "lawless passions." . . . But Daisy, on this occasion, continued to present herself as an inscrutable combination of audacity and innocence. (32)

Winterbourne swings first one way and then the other. He sides with Mrs. Walker in advising Daisy to "get into the carriage," eliciting Daisy's disdainful condemnation, "I never heard anything so stiff!" (34). But once he has entered the carriage himself, he takes Daisy's side, assuring Mrs. Walker that "I suspect she meant no harm" and that "[t]he poor girl's only fault . . . is that she is very uncultivated" (35). If anything, one would suppose that by the end of the chapter his perplexity has deepened,

for having defended Daisy to Mrs. Walker and having left her
carriage, he no sooner sees the intimacy into which Daisy and
Giovanelli have settled under the cover of her parasol than he
turns on his heel to make his way to Mrs. Costello's for yet
another attempt to assuage his bafflement in consultation with
that extremely exclusive matron.

CHAPTER 4: "AND THE MOST INNOCENT!"

We can only assume that, if Winterbourne indeed found his
aunt at home after leaving the Pincio, Mrs. Costello would have
hewed to her customary high line of condemning Daisy's behavior. That the first line in chapter 4 informs us that Winterbourne
"flattered himself on the following day that there was no smiling among the servants when he, at least, asked for Mrs. Miller
at her hotel" (36) indicates that Mrs. Costello has not succeeded
in inculcating Winterbourne with a definitive prejudice against
Daisy and that he still hopes that, as he assured Mrs. Walker on
the Pincio, "[t]here shall be nothing scandalous in my attentions
to her" (35).

At Mrs. Walker's soirée what Winterbourne feels above all
is compassion for Daisy, despite his suffering a good deal of
teasing from her about his stiffness and despite the vulgarity of
her behavior, her talking "not inaudibly" (37) during the mu-
sical performance by Giovanelli that she herself has promoted.
When he pompously tells her, "I am not sorry we can't
dance. . . . I don't dance," she replies "Of course you don't
dance; you're too stiff" (37). When he says, "I wish you would
flirt with me, and me only," she repeats the charge: "you are the
last man I should think of flirting with. As I have had the pleasure of informing you, you are too stiff" (38). Here, surely, we
have to give Daisy credit for a pointed parody of Winterbourne's stiff formalism, her "As I have had the pleasure of informing you" echoing such Winterbourne speeches as "I have

the pleasure of knowing your son" (18) and "I have had the honour of telling you that I have only just stepped out of the train" (30). When Winterbourne flashes anger at the charge of stiffness, Daisy glows with pleasure, for she has only been trying to get him to unbend a little: "Daisy gave a delighted laugh. 'If I could have the sweet hope of making you angry, I would say it again'" (38). In the course of their conversation, Daisy also offers some of what I have interpreted in the last chapter as her conscious critiques of the sexual ideology represented by the upright American matrons. But what is most memorable in this episode is her response to Mrs. Walker's turning "her back straight upon" her when she goes to bid her hostess goodnight: "Daisy turned away, looking with a pale, grave face at the circle near the door; Winterbourne saw that, for the first moment, she was too much shocked and puzzled even for indignation. He on his side was greatly touched." His sense of the wound imparted to Daisy, conveyed in his immediate comment to Mrs. Walker, "That was very cruel" (39), is confirmed later when she says to him, apropos of being given "the cold shoulder," "I shouldn't think you would let people be so unkind!" (45).

Although Winterbourne continues to defend Daisy and to call on her frequently, and though he continues to be perplexed by her, the episodes that lead up to the climax in the Colosseum show him increasingly inclined to regard her in a harsh, negative light. Thus, in a summary of his calls on the Millers and of the regularity of Giovanelli's presence in their quarters, we read that "[h]e had a pleasant sense that he should never be afraid of Daisy Miller. It must be added that this sentiment was not al-together flattering to Daisy; it was part of his conviction, or rather of his apprehension, that she would prove a very light young person" (40). When he discusses Daisy with Mrs. Cos-tello at St. Peter's, he does not advert to his belief in Daisy's innocence, merely asserting that there is nothing "to be called an intrigue," that in his view Daisy and Giovanelli do not think of marrying each other, and that Giovanelli cannot practically believe that Daisy will marry him since "[h]e has nothing but his handsome face to offer, and there is a substantial Mr. Miller in that mysterious land of dollars" (41). On this occasion, furthermore, "Winterbourne was not pleased" to hear the "great deal" that is said by "Mrs. Costello and her friends . . . about poor little Miss Miller's going really 'too far.' . . . But . . . he could not deny to himself that she was going very far indeed. He felt very sorry for her—not exactly that he believed that she had completely lost her head, but because it was painful to hear so much that was pretty and undefended and natural assigned to a vulgar place among the categories of disorder" (42). Stung, finally, by the report of a friend of having seen Daisy and Giovanelli together in the Doria Palace, Winterbourne rushes to see Mrs. Miller alone, hoping, no doubt, to stir her into taking a role properly protective of Daisy's imperiled reputation. Mrs. Miller announces that "I keep telling Daisy she's engaged," allows that Daisy "says she isn't," and confides that "I've made Mr. Giovanelli promise to tell me, if *she* doesn't. I should want to write to Mr. Miller about it—shouldn't you?" Winterbourne simply despairs: "Daisy's mamma struck him as so unprecedented in the annals of parental vigilance that he gave up as utterly irrelevant the attempt to place her upon her guard" (43).

Thereafter, the real ostracism of Daisy Miller takes hold, while Winterbourne continues to straddle the fence. He ceases to see Daisy because she is "never at home" and because the people whose society Winterbourne frequents have "ceased to invite her," intimating "that they desired to express to observant Europeans the great truth that, though Miss Daisy Miller was a young American lady, her behaviour was not representative—was regarded by her compatriots as abnormal." Winterbourne cannot tell if Daisy is too provincial "even to have perceived" her ostracism or if she has "a defiant, passionate, perfectly observant consciousness of the impression she produced," and he is still hung up on the old questions of whether she is innocent or "a young person of the reckless class," whether "her eccentricities were generic, national" or "personal." In any case, he assumes the worst, that she has been "'carried away' by Mr. Giovanelli" (43). In this conclusion, we see Winterbourne's imagination of the illicit still powerfully at work. As Lauren Cowdery comments, "Why 'carried away'? Winterbourne assumes that any man in favor would do what he was inclined to do; perhaps, in the world of this tale, he might be right."[95] At their last meeting before the Colosseum encounter, "in that beautiful abode of flowering desolation known as the Palace of the Caesars" (43), Daisy again twits Winterbourne for his stiffness and teases him about whether she is engaged. Winterbourne also senses that "Giovanelli would find a certain mental relief in being able to have a private understanding with him" (44), an intuition that looks forward to Giovanelli's words to Winterbourne by Daisy's grave.

When Winterbourne finds Daisy seated at the base of the cross in the center of the Colosseum, close to midnight and with Giovanelli in attendance, his doubts about Daisy crystallize in his single greatest error of vision. Since the beginning of his perplexity about Daisy, his unthinking male chauvinism has placed on her the burden of proving her innocence. Now, however, hearing Daisy's voice speaking in words that, ironically, reinforce for the reader a belief in her innocence and in Winterbourne's role as the despoiler thereof—"Well, he looks at us as one of the old lions or tigers may have looked at the Christian martyrs!"—Winterbourne feels with an odd mixture of horror and satisfaction that he has the answer to the puzzle: "Winterbourne stopped, with a sort of horror; and, it must be added, with a sort of relief. It was as if a sudden illumination had been flashed upon the ambiguity of Daisy's behaviour and the riddle had become easy to read. She was a young lady whom a gentleman need no longer be at pains to respect" (46). In the rest of this climactic scene, while Winterbourne *is* at pains to express a gentlemanly protectiveness about Daisy's exposure to possible infection at the Colosseum, his line toward Daisy, both in his thoughts and in his words to her, is harshly dismissive. When he starts to leave without acknowledging Daisy and Giovanelli, causing Daisy to exclaim, "Why, it was Mr. Winterbourne! He saw me—and he cuts me!", Winterbourne thinks, "What a clever little reprobate she was, and how smartly she played at injured innocence!" (46). When Daisy asks whether he now believes that she is engaged, Winterbourne's reply is withering: "I believe that it makes very little difference whether you are engaged or not!" (47). This elicits Daisy's pathetic response (her last speech in the tale if one does not count Mrs. Miller's quoting her in delivering her deathbed message to Winterbourne): "'I don't care,' said Daisy, in a little strange tone, 'whether I have Roman fever or not!'" (48).

In the Colosseum scene Winterbourne is outraged that Giovanelli has not been as protective of Daisy as convention dictated a gentleman should be of a young woman. From Winterbourne's point of view, Giovanelli has been careless of Daisy's reputation and now is being recklessly careless of her health:

> ". . . I wonder," he added, turning to Giovanelli, "that you, a native Roman, should countenance such a terrible indiscretion."
> "Ah," said the handsome native, "for myself, I am not afraid."
> "Neither am I—for you! I am speaking for this young lady."
> Giovanelli lifted his well-shaped eyebrows and showed his brilliant teeth. But he took Winterbourne's rebuke with docility. "I told the Signorina it was a grave indiscretion; but when was the Signorina ever prudent?" (47)

At the same time, I cannot help observing that in her determination to enjoy the Colosseum by moonlight ("I shouldn't have wanted to go home without that" [47]) Daisy exhibits a romantic interest in ancient monuments that we have not seen in her earlier, that redounds to her credit (in contrast to her earlier, superficial preference for society and dancing over the cultural opportunities Rome offers), and that somehow links her to Winterbourne, who has entered the Colosseum in a high ro-

mantic mood, murmuring "Byron's famous lines" (46). Winterbourne, of course, tempers his romanticism with prudence, and
he does not get through the Byron before he remembers "that if
nocturnal meditations in the Colosseum are recommended by
the poets, they are deprecated by the doctors." He is prepared
for "a hasty retreat" (46). Daisy, on the other hand, has sat out
in the "villainous miasma" (46) "[a]ll the evening" (47). Had
she been under proper parental protection, she would never
have been exposed to the disease. F. W. Dupee remarks, "Daisy's
death, if it proves anything, proves that not every superstition
is a fraud." But Daisy's imprudence, her mother's abrogation of
supervision, and the actuality of malaria in her case cannot
wholly absolve Winterbourne of culpability in her death. For if
"[h]er love for Winterbourne" is, as Dupee argues, "the one
clear impulse in her nature," then his words to her at the Colosseum can only be devastating, and it should not be hard for
us, in an age in which medical science recognizes emotional fac-
tors in the body's ability to combat disease, to see her as falling
into a long line of James protagonists who succumb to deaths
from physical causes when they are weakened by emotional
wounds, specifically by disappointment in love. These include
the heroes of such early tales as "The Story of a Year" (1865)
and "A Most Extraordinary Case" (1868) and the heroine of
one of the great works that closed James's career as a novelist,
The Wings of the Dove (1902).[96]

From the Colosseum the tale moves swiftly to its denouement. Daisy's midnight indiscretion becomes the talk of "the
little American circle" and of the hotel servants, "low-minded
menials," but for Winterbourne "it had ceased to be a matter of
serious regret." His compassion is stirred, however, by the news
that Daisy is "alarmingly ill" (48), whereupon he calls on the
Millers for more news. Since Mrs. Miller has at last taken an
active role in ministering to her daughter ("she was now, at
least, giving her daughter the advantage of her society" [48]),
Winterbourne finds Randolph holding forth before concerned

callers. Daisy's little brother provides us with the last strokes of broad humor in the story, declaring with unscientific jingoism, "You can't see anything here at night, except when there's a moon. In America there's always a moon!" (48). In Winterbourne's subsequent calls only once does he see Mrs. Miller, and then she delivers to him a message from Daisy: "She told me to tell you that she never was engaged to that handsome Italian. . . . I don't know why she wanted you to know; but she said to me three times—'Mind you tell Mr. Winterbourne.' And then she told me to ask if you remembered the time you went to that castle in Switzerland" (48–49). As Winterbourne tells his aunt in the closing dialogue, it has been "on his conscience that he had done her [Daisy] injustice," for at Daisy's grave Giovanelli has assured him that Daisy was not only "the most beautiful young lady I ever saw, and the most amiable," but also "the most innocent" (49). Winterbourne tells his aunt that at the time he had not understood the message from Daisy that Mrs. Miller had given him: "But I have understood it since. She would have appreciated one's esteem." "'Is that a modest way,' asked Mrs. Costello, 'of saying that she would have reciprocated one's affection?'" (49). Winterbourne does not reply, but in his repetition of his aunt's observation of the preceding summer—"I was booked to make a mistake. I have lived too long in foreign parts"—he perhaps betrays some awareness that he has not only mistaken Daisy, doing her a grave injustice, but has also thrown away for both of them what he should have recognized as a genuine opportunity for love. Nevertheless, the narrator's dry, ironic report of Winterbourne's resumption of his old routine in Geneva, in language echoing that of the second paragraph of the story, does not suggest any profound or lasting alteration in this stiff, young, Europeanized American.

8

THE REVISION OF 1909

For four years, between 1905 and 1909, Henry James worked on the twenty-four-volume selection of his works known as the New York Edition.[97] *The Novels and Tales of Henry James* (1907–9) excluded a number of James's novels, particularly several thought very fine today that are wholly set in America (*The Europeans, Washington Square,* and *The Bostonians*) and only included about half of James's 112 tales. Among these was a new version of *Daisy Miller,* which appeared with several other tales in volume 18 (1909). Although the general consensus among critics of Henry James is that the revised version is inferior to the original—and though this book has therefore presented a reading of the text of 1878–79—the changes James made are often very interesting in and of themselves and for the light they cast retrospectively, and by contrast, on the story as James first published it. Accordingly, no extended study of *Daisy Miller* can be complete without some attention to the New York Edition text.

In the first and last of the New York Edition prefaces James dwelt at some length on the process of revision. He did not "re-write": that is, he did not change the basic facts of his works, the characters, the settings, or the plots. But he did make sometimes numerous—sometimes, indeed, almost innumerable—changes in wording that effected subtle changes in tone, in emphasis, and in the intimate texture of the prose. The earliest works were revised most heavily because they were most distant from the mature style and sense of artistic possibilities with which he wished to align them, whereas the later works were already in his late manner. Although he says that "I had thought of re-writing as so difficult, and even as so absurd, as to be impossible," he determined that "[t]o revise is to see, or to look over, again—which means in the case of a written thing neither more nor less than to re-read it. . . . the act of revision, the act of seeing it again, caused whatever I looked at on any page to flower before me as into the only terms that honourably expressed it; and the 'revised' element in the present Edition is accordingly these terms, these rigid conditions of re-perusal, registered; so many close notes . . . on the particular vision of the matter itself that experience had at last made the only one possible."[98]

Two other metaphors that James used in the prefaces for his art of revision illuminate his practice. In one, he imagined himself as a reader trying to follow footsteps that had been made in the snow by the author he had formerly been: in re-reading recent works, James becomes a "docile reader" who sinks comfortably "[i]nto his very footprints [those of the author, his former self]," but in rereading much older stories and novels he found that "my exploring tread . . . had quite unlearned the old pace and found itself falling into another, which might sometimes indeed more or less agree with the original tracks, but might most often, or very nearly, break the surface in other places." In short, his "mode of motion" had changed as he had grown older.[99] The other metaphor is of a painter who "passes over his old sunk canvas" a sponge wet with varnish, the act revealing "what may still come out again" if he then applies a brush in a "criticism essentially active" and designed to bring out the "buried secrets" of the work.[100] As R. P. Blackmur sums up the matter, "He revised, as a rule, only in the sense that he re-envisaged the substance more accurately and more representatively."[101]

It is nevertheless true that scholars of James have felt that the revisions of the early novels and tales are in some cases so extensive as to have created essentially new works. This is true of the revision of *The Portrait of a Lady*, for example, which is generally judged to be a success, so that most readers today read the New York Edition text that is considered superior. In the case of *The American*, too, James's revisions appear to have created a new work, in this instance one that most readers feel is inferior to the original. One cannot say, then, that his revisions for the New York Edition were, on the whole, successful or unsuccessful. Each title within the edition must be judged in relation to its earlier version or versions. I should add, too, that while there is consensus on the superiority of the late *Portrait*, for example, and on that of the early *Daisy Miller*, there is in each of these cases a reasoned, plausible minority view that favors the earlier or the later text, as the case may be.

The first change that Henry James made in *Daisy Miller* may be taken as a key to all of the others. He changed the title. What had always been called *Daisy Miller: A Study* became simply *Daisy Miller* in the New York Edition text of 1909. In the 1909 preface James said that he could not recall the reasons for the original subtitle, "unless they may have taken account of a certain flatness in my poor little heroine's literal denomination."[102] Of the twelve definitions of the noun *study* provided in the *Oxford English Dictionary*, however, the tenth would seem to provide a number of cogent reasons for the "Study" of James's original title. A study, according to the *OED*, is

10. An artistic production executed for the sake of acquiring skill or knowledge, or to serve as a preparation for future work; a

careful preliminary sketch for a work of art, or (more usually) for some detail or portion of it; an artist's pictorial record of his observation of some object, incident, or effect, or of something that occurs to his mind, intended for his own guidance in his subsequent work. Also, occas., a drawing, painting, or piece of sculpture aiming to bring out the characteristics of the object represented, as they are revealed by especially careful observation. . . .

    b. A discourse or literary composition devoted to the detailed consideration of some question, or the minute description of some object; a literary work executed as an exercise or as an experiment in some particular style or mode of treatment.

The first part of this definition is apt because of James's frequent recourse to painterly metaphors for literary art, because *Daisy Miller: A Study* appears in retrospect indeed to have been "a preparation for future work," "a careful preliminary sketch" for James's later portraits of American girls (e.g., obviously, *The Portrait of a Lady*), and thus as a "record" that served for his "guidance in subsequent work." As an analytic critique, moreover, not only of Daisy Miller but also of the milieu in which she finds herself in Europe, of the mores, manners, and sexual politics of the American community abroad, *Daisy Miller: A Study* would seem to aim at bringing "out the characteristics of the object represented, as they are revealed by especially careful observation." The pertinent aspects of the second, literary part of this *OED* definition parallel these points, concentrating as they do on "detailed consideration" and "minute description" and on the "experimental," trial mode of a literary composition designated as a "study."

In other words, calling this tale "A Study" implied at once its experimental, preliminary, artistically practical status and its analytic aims of "careful observation" and "minute description." By the same token, stripping the tale of "A Study" and calling it just *Daisy Miller* makes it seem more finished and less critically analytical. As Lauren Cowdery observes, in her sensitive and helpful discussion of the revision, "the study seems quite simply like a piece of social criticism much more concerned with analyzing the failures of the people around Daisy than with developing the character of Daisy herself. . . . The shift in James's view of *Daisy Miller* corresponds to a shift in his attention and interest in this tale from the nature of the world to the nature of the guiltless character."[103] Indeed, James's observation in the preface that Daisy "was of course pure poetry, and had never been anything else" would seem to disavow the apparently realistic intention of the original tale.[104] The new, late title seems to imply that the revision at least will not have the analytic bite of a study; instead, it will be rich with the symbolism of a poetic tribute to Daisy in a text that comes much closer than the original to what Carol Ohmann feels obtains in both versions, the celebration of a "metaphysical ideal" (see n. 41).

In keeping with his new conception of Daisy as "pure poetry" James transformed his earlier concrete descriptions of her to more abstract, vague, nebulous ones, consonant with her new status as an idealized figure. For instance, Winterbourne's observation that Daisy "had the *tournure* of a princess" (12), which emphasizes her figure and her way of bearing herself physically, becomes his thought of "her natural elegance" (NYE, 21), which plays into the myth of Daisy as a "child of nature" without any concrete physical reference. James adds the word "charming" at least half a dozen times in the revised text, conveying the idea that Daisy casts a scarcely explicable spell over Winterbourne. Her first speech in the Colosseum is identical in both texts—"Well, he looks at us as one of the old lions or tigers may have looked at the Christian martyrs"—but in the original we read, "These were the words he heard, in the familiar accent of Miss Daisy Miller," whereas in the revision James puts it thus: "These words were winged with their accent, so that they fluttered and settled about him in the darkness like vague white doves. It was Miss Daisy Miller who had released them for flight" (NYE, 85–86). Not only does James's revision poeticize Daisy in this way, but it also makes the condemnation of her by others harsher and therefore less excusable, more culpable. Mrs. Costello no longer calls Daisy "a dreadful girl" (14); now she calls her "a horror" (NYE, 25). Winterbourne, in Daisy's words, no longer simply "cuts me" (46); now he "cuts me dead" (NYE, 86). James expands Winterbourne's realizaton at the Colosseum that "[s]he was a young lady whom a gentleman need no longer be at pains to respect" (46) into a couple of sentences in which Winterbourne's judgment becomes a gross matter of black and white: "She was a young lady about the *shades* of whose perversity a foolish puzzled gentleman need no longer trouble his head or his heart. That once questionable quantity *had* no shades—it was a mere black little blot" (NYE, 86). Throughout the revised tale, moreover, James sets up more signs that point to Daisy's innocence, so that we have a heightened sense of the depth of the error that takes her as anything but innocent. For example, on the steamer to Chillon, Daisy's "charming garrulity" (22) becomes her "charming innocent prattle" (NYE, 40). At the same time, against the onslaught of her ostracism, Daisy is presented, far less ambiguously, as a martyr to freedom, so that, for instance, Winterbourne no longer rebukes Giovanelli at the graveside for taking Daisy to the Colosseum just because she wanted to go—"That was no reason!" he exclaims in the original (49)—but instead repeats Giovanelli's words, "She did what she liked" (NYE, 92), in implicit tribute to the independent streak in Daisy for which they both have admired her.

There are far more revisions in the New York Edition than I can note in this brief study. If Winterbourne and Giovanelli seem in the revision to share a moment of communion at the graveside, musing together over Daisy's having done "what she liked," the apparent softening of the touched-up portrait of Daisy's Italian friend is counterbalanced by the way in which he is stripped of humanity when he is first introduced in the revised text. Compare the two short paragraphs below, the first of 1879, the second of 1909:

> Winterbourne perceived at some distance a little man standing
> with folded arms, nursing his cane. He had a handsome face, an
> artfully poised hat, a glass in one eye and a nosegay in his button-
> hole. Winterbourne looked at him a moment and then said, "Do
> you mean to speak to that man?" (31)

> Winterbourne descried hereupon at some distance a little figure
> that stood with folded arms and nursing its cane. It had a hand-
> some face, a hat artfully poised, a glass in one eye and a nosegay
> in its buttonhole. Daisy's friend looked at it a moment and then
> said: "Do you mean to speak to that thing?" (NYE, 56)

As Cowdery points out, James made Daisy's speech much
more vernacular and less grammatical in the revision, as if to
counterbalance the more poetic, vaguer turn of the narrator's
descriptions of her. "Thus," she observes, "as he revises Daisy's
character, James is clearly constructing a paradox," for he plays
off a "vision of Daisy as pretty, fragile, and nebulous against an
equally undeniable one of her as prosaic: ... pushy, folksy,
sharp-tongued, and more than occasionally flat-footed."[105] The
result of the paradox, of making Daisy in the revision a composition "of charming little parts that didn't match and that
made no *ensemble*" (NYE, 10), is to remove the story from the
realm of realism in which it originally operated and to reinforce
the mythic dimension of Daisy's almost magical attraction. Neither Daisy's behavior nor Winterbourne's puzzlement is any
longer, in 1909, a result of the cultural conditioning of each:
Daisy is so paradoxical as to put verisimilitude—the very quality early readers had recognized in the original Daisy—out of
the question, and we need not have recourse to Winterbourne's
European formation to explain his bewilderment in the face of
a character who is no longer so much "an American girl" as an
attempted tour de force of "pure poetry."

Many readers prefer the earlier version, *Daisy Miller: A
Study*, simply because they do not take to James's late style, to
its more complicated grammar, its sometimes exotic diction,
and its tendency to elegant elaboration. They object to the

verbal texture of a prose that leans toward such formulations as "with a certain scared obliquity" (NYE, 35) in place of "askance" (19) and to such wordy (and allegorizing) substitutions as "his little friend the child of nature of the Swiss lakeside" (NYE, 46) for a simple "Daisy Miller" (25), just as they object, in James's revision of *The American,* to the substitution of "he spoke, as to cheek and chin, of the joy of the matutinal steel" for the simple "he was clean-shaved."[106] As a reader who generally prefers James's later manner, and who has argued that his greatest works are those triumphs of the late style *The Ambassadors, The Wings of the Dove,* and *The Golden Bowl,* I must say that my objection to the revised *Daisy Miller* does not rest on such matters of verbal texture but, rather, on the view that in so heavily emphasizing Daisy's symbolic embodiment of an ideal of freedom—in so insistently poeticizing her—James greatly simplifies the story by giving clear ascendancy to what was in the earlier version one of many elements or subtexts held in true dialectical tension, taking a complex, dark comedy of manners and making it into a considerably more sentimental and one-sided piece of symbolist prose poetry.[107] In the revised *Daisy* the late style—so often elsewhere a vehicle for James's increasing complexity of vision, for his deepening appreciation of moral and psychological ambiguity—becomes the means of depriving the text of 1878–79 of its full range of ironic qualifications and complexities. Those qualifications and complexities are what I want to emphasize in the conclusion of this book, to which we are now ready to turn.

9

CONCLUSION

When Winterbourne asks Daisy Miller if she means to speak to Giovanelli (in the Pincio scene), she replies, "Do I mean to speak to him? Why, you don't suppose I mean to communicate by signs?" (31). In its immediate context Daisy's point is of course well taken, but we may also take her question—"you don't suppose I mean to communicate by signs?"—as an indication of her own failure of understanding, a failure that at least matches the errors of vision of Mrs. Costello, Mrs. Walker, and, above all, Winterbourne, and that makes her, as much as all of those others, the author of her own troubles. What Daisy fails to understand, in short, is that one communicates by signs, that signs are arbitrary and artificial, not natural, that they are conventional, not inherent in being, and that, in one's behavior as well as in one's speech, one is always communicating "by signs." Daisy's not caring about convention, therefore, can be seen in part as her not caring about communication. Others do not understand her innocence in part because they are hidebound, because they are blinded by convention and by prejudice, but also in part because Daisy fails to communicate what she really is.

She is in this respect nowhere nearly so far advanced as the considerably more intellectual heroine of *The Portrait of a Lady*, James's next great success with the "American girl," for though Isabel, like Daisy, is "ground in the very mill of the conventional" (see n. 3), she realizes that Madame Merle's "nature spoke none the less in her behaviour because it spoke a conventional language" and thereupon she asks herself, "What is language at all but a convention?"[108]

Several of the best commentators on *Daisy Miller* have recognized this failure in Daisy. F. W. Dupee, for example, says that Daisy "as a social being . . . is without a form and a frame" and that "[s]he has no sense of the inevitable—which was what traditions and taboos, conventions and manners finally signified to James."[109] Similarly, Lauren Cowdery sees Daisy's refusal to acknowledge convention, which leaves her "in no measurable relation" to the society in which she operates, as a principal cause of her isolation and as tantamount to "a refusal to recognize speech as an instrument of communication at all."[110] Another way of putting this is that Daisy fails to understand the essential premise of the very genre in which she has her fictional life, the novel of manners. In his excellent study *The Novel of Manners in America* James W. Tuttleton defines the form as "a novel in which the manners, social customs, folkways, conventions, traditions, and mores of a given social group at a given time and place play a dominant role in the lives of fictional characters, exert control over their thought and behavior, and constitute a determinant upon the actions in which they are engaged, and in which these manners and customs are detailed realistically—with, in fact, a premium upon the exactness of their representation." In a novel of manners, moreover, the subtle nuances of people's behavior express the underlying ideologies of their society and their own inner, moral being as well: as Tuttleton observes, "Sometimes morals and manners are . . . inextricably mixed. . . . in the novels of Henry James we cannot always be sure that there is any difference."[111] *Daisy Miller: A*

Study demonstrates, among many other things, that to abandon convention utterly is to imperil the very possibility of relation among human beings.

Among the subtitles I had considered for this book were "A Tragedy of Error" or "A Tragicomedy of Error." But "A Dark Comedy of Manners" seemed preferable. The word *tragedy* would suggest that in the end the protagonist—whether Daisy or Winterbourne—achieves some ennobling awareness of the meaning of what has happened and of his or her own shortcomings, and I do not believe that either of the central figures in *Daisy Miller* comes to such a recognition. A tragicomedy, by definition, is a work (usually a play) with a mainly tragic character but with a happy ending, whereas *Daisy Miller* is a work with a mainly comic character but with an unhappy ending. *Daisy Miller* is a dark comedy, in my view, not only because of its sad ending, not only because of the pathos (not the tragedy) of Daisy's death, but also because of the cultural determinism it presupposes, because not one of the characters—not Mrs. Walker and Mrs. Costello, certainly, nor Winterbourne, the most open-minded of the "conventional" characters, nor Daisy, the supposedly "natural" American girl—can overcome the environmental determinism that finally makes it impossible for Daisy and Winterbourne to meet each other halfway, she by growing beyond the crude provinciality of Schenectady and he by growing beyond the stifling proprieties of Geneva and of the American colony in Rome.

It is all too easy for us to misread Daisy through the lens of James's 1909 preface and of his late revision of the tale, and even without those late documents, our disposition today is probably to exaggerate Daisy's martyrdom, freedom, and innocence, and the brutal stupidity of those who mistakenly ostracize her. If I have emphasized in these closing remarks Daisy's culpability and the cultural determinism that entraps her as well as Winterbourne, it is as a corrective to these tendencies. Daisy is on one level, as I said at the outset of this study, an embodiment of the free spirit, but, as I said then, too, she is crippled by her own ignorance (which is the dark side of her innocence) as much as she is injured by the prejudices of other people and by the repressive, hurtful ideology of her society. Thus *Daisy Miller* remains (again in Richard Hocks's phrase [see n. 13]) "a true dialectical inquiry." Even in this early and comparatively simple work James was looking all around his subject, was not seeing it from a single side, and was in fact fulfilling his own injunction to would-be novelists in "The Art of Fiction": he was trying, with famous success, "to be one of the people on whom nothing is lost."[112]

NOTES

1. Rebecca West, *Henry James* (New York: Henry Holt & Co., 1916), 46–47. For an account of the immediate success of *Daisy Miller* and of James's sudden celebrity in London, see Leon Edel, *Henry James, The Conquest of London: 1870–1881,* vol. 2 of *The Life of Henry James* (Philadelphia and New York: J. B. Lippincott, 1962), 303–4, 308–12, and 327–40.

2. *Henry James Letters: 1875–1883,* vol. 2 of *Henry James Letters,* ed. Leon Edel (Cambridge, Mass.: Harvard University Press, 1975), 150–51.

3. *The Complete Notebooks of Henry James,* ed. Leon Edel and Lyall H. Powers (New York: Oxford University Press, 1987), 13.

4. For important treatments of the myth of the American girl, see Paul John Eakin, *The New England Girl: Cultural Ideals in Hawthorne, Stowe, Howells and James* (Athens: University of Georgia Press, 1976), and Virginia C. Fowler, *Henry James's American Girl: The Embroidery on the Canvas* (Madison: University of Wisconsin Press, 1984). For Leslie Fiedler's view of the treatment of women in classic American fiction, see his *An End to Innocence: Essays on Culture and Politics* (Boston: Beacon Press, 1955), esp. chaps. 9 ("Come Back to the Raft Ag'in, Huck Honey!") and 13 ("Adolescence and Maturity in the American Novel").

5. *Hawthorne* (1879), in *Literary Criticism: Essays on Literature, American Writers, English Writers,* ed. Leon Edel (New York: Library of America, 1984), 350–51.

6. William James, quoted in F. O. Matthiessen, *The James Family, Including Selections from the Writings of Henry James, Senior, William, Henry, and Alice James* (New York: Alfred A. Knopf, 1947), 69.

7. Recent studies of the James family have emphasized that in many respects Henry James, Sr., exercised a subtle tyranny over his children despite his professed devotion to freedom. In addition, biographical studies of the tragedy of Alice James have suggested that it was much harder to be a girl in that family than to be a boy. See Howard Feinstein, *Becoming William James* (Ithaca, N.Y.: Cornell University Press, 1984); Alfred Habegger, *Henry James*

and the *"Woman Business"* (Cambridge: Cambridge University Press, 1989); Jean Strouse, *Alice James: A Life* (Boston: Houghton Mifflin, 1980); and Ruth Bernard Yeazell, *The Death and Letters of Alice James* (Berkeley: University of California Press, 1981).

8. Matthiessen, *The James Family,* 70.

9. Ibid., 321.

10. Ezra Pound, "Henry James," in *Instigations* (New York: Boni & Liveright, 1920), 107–8. Pound's remarks here are reprinted from his Introduction to the special Henry James number of the *Little Review* (August 1918).

11. See Theodora Bosanquet, "The Revised Version," *Little Review* 5 (August 1918):57.

12. Preface to *Daisy Miller, Pandora, The Patagonia, and Other Tales,* vol. 18 of the New York Edition of *The Novels and Tales of Henry James* (New York: Charles Scribner's Sons, 1909), vi; this edition hereafter cited as NYE in notes and parenthetically in the text.

13. Richard A. Hocks, *"Daisy Miller,* Backward into the Past: A Centennial Essay," *Henry James Review* 1 (1980):178.

14. Lauren T. Cowdery, *The Nouvelle of Henry James in Theory and Practice* (Ann Arbor, Mich.: UMI Research Press, 1986), 80, 82.

15. For a study that sees this configuration of the free spirit in conflict with the world as "the figure in the carpet" in James's fiction, see Daniel J. Schneider, *The Crystal Cage: Adventures of the Imagination in the Fiction of Henry James* (Lawrence: Regents Press of Kansas, 1978).

16. Preface to *Daisy Miller,* NYE, v–vi.

17. "The Contributor's Club," *Atlantic Monthly* 43 (February 1879):258 and (March 1879):399.

18. For corrections of the misattributions to Howells, see two notes by George Monteiro, "William Dean Howells: Two Mistaken Attributions," *Papers of the Bibliographical Society of America* 56 (1962):254–57, and "'Girlhood on the American Plan'—A Contemporary Defense of *Daisy Miller,"* *Books at Brown* 19 (May 1963):89–93. Unfortunately, Monteiro's notes appeared too late to keep the misattributions from being perpetuated in one of the most useful collections of documentary materials on *Daisy Miller,* William T. Stafford's *James's Daisy Miller: The Story, the Play, the Critics* (New York: Charles Scribner's Sons, 1963). Stafford's volume, which includes the *Cornhill* text of *Daisy Miller* and the script of James's play *Daisy Miller: A Comedy in Three Acts,* along with a variety of critical comments on both, begins a compilation of Howells's comments on the tale (110–14) with excerpts from the two "Contributor's Club" columns.

19. Howells to Lowell, 22 June 1879, in *Life in Letters of William Dean Howells,* ed. Mildred Howells, 2 vols. (New York: Doubleday, Doran, 1928), 1:271.

Notes

20. Edmund L. Volpe, "The Reception of *Daisy Miller*," *Boston Public Library Quarterly* 10 (January 1958):55–59.

21. Edel, *Henry James, The Conquest of London*, 308–9. The legend, it seems, dies extraordinarily hard. It is repeated by instructors in countless classrooms, abetted, no doubt, by such recent authority as this note in a Norton Critical Edition: "This letter [Henry James to Mrs. F. H. Hill, 21 March 1879] was written at a moment when James was being sharply criticized in the United States for having committed an 'outrage' on American girlhood in his portrait of Daisy Miller" (*Tales of Henry James*, ed. Christof Wegelin [New York: W. W. Norton, 1984], 385).

22. *New York Times* editorial, 4 June 1879, 4.

23. "The Art of Fiction," in *Literary Criticism: Essays on Literature, American Writers, English Writers*, 46, 63.

24. Unsigned review of *Daisy Miller, New York Times*, 10 November 1878, 10; "Recent Novels," *Nation* 27 (19 December 1878):387; Richard Grant White, "Recent Fiction," *North American Review* 128 (January 1879):106.

25. See Elizabeth F. Hoxie, "Mrs. Grundy Adopts Daisy Miller," *New England Quarterly* 19 (December 1946):474–84.

26. William Dean Howells, "Henry James, Jr.," *Century Magazine* 25 (November 1882):25–26.

27. William Dean Howells, "Mr. James's Daisy Miller," in *Heroines of Fiction*, 2 vols. (New York: Harper & Bros., 1901), 2:164, 165–66, 170, 175–76.

28. For a succinct discussion of the New Critics' view of the intentional fallacy, see "Intentional Fallacy," in M. H. Abrams, *A Glossary of Critical Terms*, 5th ed. (New York: Holt, Rinehart & Winston, 1988).

29. For an example of the contemporary insistence that all critics are theorists, consciously or unconsciously, see Terry Eagleton, *Literary Theory: An Introduction* (Minneapolis: University of Minnesota Press, 1983).

30. *Henry James Letters, 1875–1883*, 303–4.

31. Kenneth Graham, *Henry James, The Drama of Fulfillment: An Approach to the Novels* (Oxford: Clarendon Press, 1975), n. 10, 23.

32. Preface to *Daisy Miller*, NYE, v–viii.

33. Viola Dunbar, "A Note on the Genesis of *Daisy Miller*," *Philological Quarterly* 27 (April 1948):184–86; Edward Stone, "A Further Note on *Daisy Miller* and Cherbuliez," *Philological Quarterly* 29 (April 1950):213–16; Motley Deakin, "Daisy Miller, Tradition, and the European Heroine," *Comparative Literature Studies* 6 (March 1969):45–59. See also Eva Kagan-Kans, "Ivan Turgenev and Henry James: *First Love* and *Daisy Miller*," in *American Contributions to the Ninth International Conference of Slavists, Kiev, September, 1983, II: Literature, Poetics, History*, ed. Paul Debreczeny (Columbus, Ohio: Slavica, 1983), 251–65.

34. For discussions of James's relation to Hawthorne, see, especially, Watson Branch, "'The Deeper Psychology': James's Legacy from Hawthorne," *Arizona Quarterly* 40 (Spring 1984):67–74, and Robert Emmet Long, *The Great Succession: Henry James and the Legacy of Hawthorne* (Pittsburgh: University of Pittsburgh Press, 1979), esp. 54–67.

35. Carl Wood, "Frederick Winterbourne, James's Prisoner of Chillon," *Studies in the Novel* 9 (1977):33–45.

36. Motley Deakin, "Two Studies of *Daisy Miller*," *Henry James Review* 5 (Fall 1983):2–28.

37. Adeline R. Tintner, "Two Innocents in Rome: Daisy Miller and Innocent the Tenth," *Essays in Literature* 6 (1979):71–78; Jeffrey Meyers, "Velázquez and *Daisy Miller*," *Studies in Short Fiction* 16 (1979):171–78.

38. Viola Dunbar, "The Revision of *Daisy Miller*," *Modern Language Notes* 65 (May 1950):311–17; Dee Hansen Ohi, "The Limits of Revision: Henry James's Rewriting of *Daisy Miller: A Study*," dissertation, University of Denver, 1981.

39. W. M. Gibson and G. R. Petty, "Project *Occult*: The Ordered Computer Collation of Unprepared Literary Text," in *Art and Error: Modern Textual Editing*, ed. Ronald Gottesman and Scott Boyce Bennett (Bloomington: Indiana University Press, 1970), 279–300.

40. Frederick Newberry, "A Note on the Horror in James's Revision of *Daisy Miller*," *Henry James Review* 3 (Spring 1982):229–32.

41. Carol Ohmann, "Daisy Miller: A Study of Changing Intentions," *American Literature* 36 (March 1964):1–11.

42. See Cowdery's chap. 5 in *The Nouvelle of Henry James*, 73–94, and Mary Doyle Springer, *Forms of the Modern Novella* (Chicago: University of Chicago Press, 1975).

43. The early, idealizing view is apparent, for example, in two of the first book-length studies of James, Rebecca West's *Henry James* and Cornelia Pulsifer Kelley's *The Early Development of Henry James* (Urbana: University of Illinois Press, 1930).

44. See n. 13.

45. Wayne C. Booth, *The Rhetoric of Fiction* (Chicago: University of Chicago Press, 1961), 282–84; James W. Gargano, "*Daisy Miller*: An Abortive Quest for Innocence," *South Atlantic Quarterly* 59 (1960):114–20; John H. Randall, "The Genteel Reader and *Daisy Miller*," *American Quarterly* 17 (1965):568–81; R. P. Draper, "Death of a Hero? Winterbourne and Daisy Miller," *Studies in Short Fiction* 6 (1969):601–8; Ian Kennedy, "Frederick Winterbourne: The Good Bad Boy in *Daisy Miller*," *Arizona Quarterly* 29 (1973):139–50; William E. Grant, "*Daisy Miller*: A Study of a Study," *Studies in Short Fiction* 11 (1974):17–25; Cathy N. Davidson, "'Circumsexualocution' in Henry James's *Daisy Miller*," *Arizona Quarterly* 32 (1976):353–66. C. Hugh Holman's discussion of Winterbourne as the hero of a typically

American bildungsroman also belongs with these Winterbourne-centered readings; see his *Windows on the World: Essays on American Social Fiction* (Knoxville: University of Tennessee Press, 1979).

46. See F. W. Dupee, *Henry James* (New York: William Sloan, 1951), 106–13, and Edel, *Henry James, The Conquest of London*, 306–8.

47. Kristian Pruitt McColgan, *Henry James, 1917–1959: A Reference Guide* (Boston: G. K. Hall, 1979); Dorothy M. Scura, *Henry James, 1960–1974: A Reference Guide* (Boston: G. K. Hall, 1979).

48. Motley Deakin provides this tally in note 9 to his "Two Studies of *Daisy Miller*" (see n. 36). My discussion of voice and style in *Daisy Miller* is generally indebted to Deakin's excellent treatment of these matters in "Two Studies," particularly pp. 17–19.

49. See n. 27.

50. Deakin, "Two Studies of *Daisy Miller*," 18.

51. Ibid., 19.

52. The locus classicus for such an understanding of the artificial status of fictional narrators is Wayne Booth's *Rhetoric of Fiction* (see n. 45).

53. Cowdery, *The Nouvelle of Henry James*, 94.

54. Preface to *Daisy Miller*, NYE, v. In one of the best discussions of Daisy's name, Richard Hocks suggests that she may also be connected, ironically, with the European species of the plant, "commonly referred to as 'bachelor's button,' suggesting, as boutonniere, a number of images antithetical to Daisy's free-spiritedness and natural state, indeed suggesting elements of conformity, of unlimbered rigidity, of exactness and precision, all by dint of being severed from the natural soil." See Hocks's "*Daisy Miller*, Backward into the Past," 174, and also, for another discussion of the names in the story, William E. Grant's "*Daisy Miller*: A Study of a Study" (n. 45).

55. All of these definitions are given in *The Dictionary of American Slang*, comp. Harold Wentworth and Stuart Berg Flexner (New York: Thomas Y. Crowell, 1975), 138. The same source notes that "push up the daisies" has been used to mean "buried in one's grave" since about 1860 (413).

56. Theodore Dreiser, *Sister Carrie*, ed. Neda M. Westlake et al. (Philadelphia: University of Pennsylvania Press, 1981), 57.

57. Elsdon C. Smith, *New Dictionary of American Family Names* (New York: Harper & Row, 1973), 555.

58. *Daisy Miller*, NYE, vol. 18, 31.

59. Karl Baedeker, *Switzerland: Handbook for Travellers* (Leipzig: Karl Baedeker, 1879), 202.

60. Ibid., 205; for Byron's sonnet and his note on "The Prisoner of Chillon" (titled "Advertisement"), see *The Poetical Works of Lord Byron* (London: Oxford University Press, 1921), 326.

61. *Transatlantic Sketches* (Boston: James R. Osgood, 1875), 66.

62. Baedeker, *Switzerland*, 203.

63. Karl Baedeker, *Italy: Handbook for Travellers; Second Part: Central Italy and Rome* (Leipzig: Karl Baedeker, 1897), 141.

64. A. Gallenga, *Italy Revisited*, 2 vols. (London: Samuel Tinsley, 1876), 7:41–42.

65. *Transatlantic Sketches*, 197–99.

66. See Manfred's speech that opens act 3, scene 4, *The Poetical Works of Lord Byron*, 394–95.

67. Ibid., 238; Carl Maves, *Sensuous Pessimism: Italy in the Work of Henry James* (Bloomington: Indiana University Press, 1973), 60. Maves quotes other lines from the many stanzas on the Colosseum in *Childe Harold,* noting that Byron's apostrophe to Time as "The beautifier of the dead . . . the corrector where our judgments err" forecasts that "death does indeed 'beautify' her [Daisy] for Winterbourne by correcting his original, coldly cautious judgment of her."

68. Deakin, "Two Studies of *Daisy Miller*," 13. The first of Deakin's "Two Studies," "Daisy Miller and Baedeker," is a mine of information on the nineteenth-century associations of the settings of the story and on their implications for interpreting it. Deakin includes copious data on matters not covered in the present brief discussion, on, for instance, the Hôtel des Trois Couronnes.

69. Ibid., 16. For a description of the cemetery in which James pays tribute to Shelley and to Keats, see his "The After-Season in Rome" in *Transatlantic Sketches*, 185–87.

70. For a scholarly essay that persuasively argues that James alluded to the centennial and to the Revolution for similar purposes in a story he wrote shortly after *Daisy Miller* with the idea of following up on its great success, see Adeline R. Tintner, "'An International Episode': A Centennial Review of a Centennial Story," *Henry James Review* 1 (1979):24–60.

71. *Daisy Miller*, NYE, 86.

72. Baedeker, *Italy: Handbook for Travellers*, xxv, 247.

73. Edel, *Henry James: The Conquest of London*, 308.

74. Harvey Green, *The Light of the Home: An Intimate View of the Lives of Women in Victorian America* (New York: Pantheon Books, 1983), 12.

75. Unsigned, "The Contributor's Club," *Atlantic Monthly* 43 (March 1879):400. For the attribution to Hay see n. 17.

76. Pat Jalland, *Women, Marriage and Politics, 1860–1914* (Oxford: Clarendon Press, 1986), 24–25.

77. Ibid., 8.

78. Mary, Countess of Lovelace, "Society and the Season," in *Fifty Years, Memoirs and Contrasts: A Composite Picture of the Period 1882–*

1932, by Twenty-Seven Contributors to the "Times" (London: T. Butterworth, 1932), 37.

79. *The Portrait of a Lady* in *Novels 1881–1886: Washington Square, The Portrait of a Lady, The Bostonians,* ed. William T. Stafford (New York: Library of America, 1985), 501.

80. Hocks, "*Daisy Miller,* Backward into the Past," 172–73.

81. Cowdery, *The Nouvelle of Henry James,* 80–82.

82. Edward Wagenknecht, *The Tales of Henry James* (New York: Frederick Ungar, 1984), 219, n. 8.

83. Green, *The Light of the Home,* 12.

84. *The Portrait of a Lady,* 258–59.

85. Hocks, "*Daisy Miller,* Backward into the Past," 173; see also *Henry James Letters, 1843–1875,* vol. 1 of *Henry James Letters,* 208.

86. Cowdery in *The Nouvelle of Henry James,* 80, points out Daisy's offense against Winterbourne's "sense of caste."

87. The most important and influential formulators of the ideas contained in James's prefaces are Joseph Warren Beach in *The Method of Henry James* (New Haven, Conn.: Yale University Press, 1918), Percy Lubbock in *The Craft of Fiction* (New York: Charles Scribner's Sons, 1921), and Richard P. Blackmur in his long introduction to his collection of the prefaces, *The Art of the Novel: Critical Prefaces by Henry James* (New York: Charles Scribner's Sons, 1934).

88. "On Henry James," the brief essay containing Eliot's famous comment, first appeared in the special Henry James number of the *Little Review* (August 1918) and is reprinted in *The Question of Henry James,* ed. F. W. Dupee (New York: Henry Holt, 1945).

89. The resonance of *grave* deepens, incidentally, when Giovanelli says of Daisy's determination to spend time at the Colosseum at night despite the risk of infection, "I told the Signorina it was a grave indiscretion" (47).

90. Edel, *Henry James, The Conquest of London,* 306.

91. The Norton Critical Edition cited throughout this book contains a typographical error in this quotation, giving "ask" for "asked." In quoting the line, I have corrected the mistake. It is a commonplace of bibliography that every typesetting of a work will introduce new errors into the text. Two others that I have noticed in the Norton Critical Edition are question marks where there should simply be periods on p. 14, line 1, and on p. 31, line 22.

92. Hocks, "*Daisy Miller,* Backward into the Past," 177.

93. *Henry James Letters, 1843–1875,* 160.

94. To William James, 27 December 1869, ibid., 179.

95. Cowdery, *The Nouvelle of Henry James,* 82.

96. F. W. Dupee, *Henry James,* rev. ed. (Garden City, N.Y.: Doubleday, 1956), 94–95.

97. In 1917, after James's death, two more volumes were issued, the hitherto unpublished and unfinished novels *The Sense of the Past* and *The Ivory Tower*, bringing the complete edition to twenty-six volumes.

98. Preface to *The Golden Bowl*, in *The Art of the Novel*, ed. Blackmur, 338–39.

99. Ibid., 336.

100. Preface to *Roderick Hudson*, ibid., 77.

101. Blackmur, introduction to *The Art of the Novel*, xxvi.

102. Preface to *Daisy Miller*, NYE, vi.

103. Cowdery, *The Nouvelle of Henry James*, 84.

104. Preface to *Daisy Miller*, NYE, viii.

105. Cowdery, *The Nouvelle of Henry James*, 78–79.

106. The long and the short descriptions of Newman's physiognomy in *The American* may be found in the second paragraphs of any texts that reproduce, respectively, the New York Edition revision and the original version of the novel.

107. I treat the late novels at length in my *Henry James and the Structure of the Romantic Imagination* (Baton Rouge: Louisiana State University Press, 1981).

108. *The Portrait of a Lady*, 388.

109. Dupee, *Henry James*, 94.

110. Cowdery, *The Nouvelle of Henry James*, 86.

111. James W. Tuttleton, *The Novel of Manners in America* (Chapel Hill: University of North Carolina Press, 1972), 10, 12.

112. "The Art of Fiction," in *Literary Criticism*, 53.

SELECTED BIBLIOGRAPHY

Primary Works

Editions of *Daisy Miller*

Daisy Miller: A Study, in Two Parts. Cornhill Magazine 37 (June 1878):678–98; 38 (July 1878):44–67. The original publication.

Daisy Miller: A Study. In *Daisy Miller/An International Episode/Four Meetings.* New York: Harper & Bros., 1878. The first American edition, published in 1878, and unsupervised by Henry James.

Daisy Miller: A Study. In *Daisy Miller/An International Episode/Four Meetings.* London: Macmillan & Co., 1879. The first English edition, for which James read proof.

Daisy Miller. In *Daisy Miller, Pandora, The Patagonia, and Other Tales.* Vol. 18 of the New York Edition of *The Novels and Tales of Henry James.* New York: Charles Scribner's Sons, 1909. The late, revised text of the tale.

Daisy Miller: A Study. In vol. 3 of *The Tales of Henry James.* Edited by Maqbool Aziz. New York: Oxford University Press, 1984. An appendix collates variants of the *Cornhill* version, the 1879 Macmillan version, and the 1909 New York Edition text.

Daisy Miller: A Study. In *Tales of Henry James.* Edited by Christof Wegelin. New York: W. W. Norton, 1984. A reprint of the 1879 Macmillan edition, cited parenthetically throughout this book.

Other Works by Henry James

"The Art of Fiction." In *Literary Criticism: Essays on Literature, American Writers, English Writers,* edited by Leon Edel, 44–65. New York: Library of America, 1984.

The Art of the Novel: Critical Prefaces by Henry James. Edited by Richard P. Blackmur. New York: Charles Scribner's Sons, 1934.

The Complete Notebooks of Henry James. Edited by Leon Edel and Lyall H. Powers. New York: Oxford University Press, 1987.

Hawthorne. In *Literary Criticism: Essays on Literature, American Writers, English Writers,* edited by Leon Edel, 315–457. New York: Library of America, 1984.

Henry James Letters. Edited by Leon Edel. 4 vols. Cambridge, Mass.: Harvard University Press, 1974–84. The most complete modern edition, these volumes nevertheless contain only about six percent of James's extant correspondence.

The Portrait of a Lady. In *Novels 1881–1886: Washington Square, The Portrait of a Lady, The Bostonians.* Edited by William T. Stafford. New York: Library of America, 1985.

Preface. In *Daisy Miller, Pandora, The Patagonia, and Other Tales,* v–xxiv. Vol. 18 of the New York Edition of *The Novels and Tales of Henry James.* New York: Charles Scribner's Sons, 1909.

Transatlantic Sketches. Boston: James R. Osgood, 1875.

Secondary Works

Books

Beach, Joseph Warren. *The Method of Henry James.* New Haven, Conn.: Yale University Press, 1918. A pioneering study of James's innovations in fictional technique.

Booth, Wayne C. *The Rhetoric of Fiction.* Chicago: University of Chicago Press, 1961. Includes astute comments on James's use of the point-of-view character in *Daisy.*

Cowdery, Lauren T. *The Nouvelle of Henry James in Theory and Practice.* Ann Arbor, Mich.: UMI Research Press, 1986. Contains an excellent chapter on *Daisy Miller,* focused on the contrast between the original "study" and the revised "*nouvelle.*"

Dupee, F. W. *Henry James.* New York: William Sloan, 1951. The best short, one-volume critical biography.

———, ed. *The Question of Henry James.* New York: Henry Holt, 1945. An important collection of essays that spurred the greatly increased critical interest in Henry James after World War II.

Eakin, Paul John. *The New England Girl: Cultural Ideals in Hawthorne, Stowe, Howells and James*. Athens: University of Georgia Press, 1976. Contains material on Daisy Miller and on James's other "American girls."

Edel, Leon. *The Life of Henry James*. 5 vols. Philadelphia: J. B. Lippincott, 1953–1972. The definitive modern scholarly biography.

Feinstein, Howard. *Becoming William James*. Ithaca, N.Y.: Cornell University Press, 1984. Provides insight into what it meant to grow up in the James family.

Fiedler, Leslie. *Love and Death in the American Novel*. New York: Criterion Books, 1960. Includes brief, influential remarks on Daisy as "the Good Bad Girl," an archetypal American character "with her heart of truest gold beneath the roughest of exteriors."

Fogel, Daniel Mark. *Henry James and the Structure of the Romantic Imagination*. Baton Rouge: Louisiana State University Press, 1981. Includes brief comments on the dialectical ordonnance of *Daisy Miller*.

Fowler, Virginia C. *Henry James's American Girl: The Embroidery on the Canvas*. Madison: University of Wisconsin Press, 1984. A study of the evolution of this character type in James's work.

Graham, Kenneth. *Henry James, the Drama of Fulfillment: An Approach to the Novels*. Oxford: Clarendon Press, 1975. The second half of chapter 1 concentrates on interpreting *Daisy Miller*.

Green, Harvey. *The Light of the Home: An Intimate View of the Lives of Women in Victorian America*. New York: Pantheon Books, 1983. Casts light on American courtship practices and on the manners of young women in Daisy Miller's time.

Habegger, Alfred. *Henry James and the "Woman Business."* Cambridge: Cambridge University Press, 1989. A critical exploration of James's view of women's issues and sexual politics.

Hoffman, Charles G. *The Short Novels of Henry James*. New York: Bookman Associates, 1957. Treats *Daisy Miller* as a series of "contrasts in atmosphere, scene and character."

Holman, C. Hugh. *Windows on the World: Essays on American Social Fiction*. Knoxville: University of Tennessee Press, 1979. Discusses *Daisy Miller* as a typical American bildungsroman with Winterbourne as the protagonist.

Howells, William Dean. *Life in Letters of William Dean Howells*. Edited by Mildred Howells. 2 vols. New York: Doubleday, Doran, 1928. Contains Howells's comments on *Daisy Miller* in his letter to James Russell Lowell, 22 June 1879.

———. *Heroines of Fiction*. 2 vols. New York: Harper & Bros., 1901. Vol. 2 includes Howells's essay "Mr. James's Daisy Miller."

Jalland, Pat. *Women, Marriage, and Politics, 1860–1914*. Oxford: Clarendon

Press, 1986. The first two chapters give a good idea of the education and regulation of young women in England and on the Continent in James's time.

Kelley, Cornelia Pulsifer. *The Early Development of Henry James*. Urbana: University of Illinois Press, 1930. An important early study that exemplifies idealized conceptions of Daisy's character.

Kraft, James. *The Early Tales of Henry James*. Carbondale: Southern Illinois University Press, 1955. Emphasizes the mythic (as opposed to realistic) dimension of *Daisy Miller*.

Long, Robert Emmet. *The Great Succession: Henry James and the Legacy of Hawthorne*. Pittsburgh: University of Pittsburgh Press, 1979. Discusses *Daisy* with respect to James's response to his greatest American precursor, Hawthorne.

Lubbock, Percy. *The Craft of Fiction*. New York: Charles Scribner's Sons, 1921. An influential, systematic formulation of the theory of fiction implicit in James's New York Edition prefaces.

Matthiesson, F. O. *The James Family, Including Selections from the Writings of Henry James, Senior, William, Henry, and Alice James*. New York: Alfred A. Knopf, 1947. Important commentary and a rich collection of documentary materials.

Maves, Carl. *Sensuous Pessimism: Italy in the Works of Henry James*. Bloomington: Indiana University Press, 1973. Treats *Daisy Miller* with emphasis on its use of the Italian setting, characters, and literary associations.

Ohi, Dee Hansen. "The Limits of Revision: Henry James's Rewriting of Daisy Miller: A Study." Dissertation, University of Denver, 1981. A full-length study of James's revision of *Daisy*.

Putt, S. Gorley. *Henry James: A Reader's Guide*. Ithaca, N.Y.: Cornell University Press, 1966. Useful as the only critical book that treats every one of James's stories and novels.

Schneider, Daniel J. *The Crystal Cage: Adventures of the Imagination in the Fiction of Henry James*. Lawrence: Regents Press of Kansas, 1978. Sees the struggle of the free spirit against an enslaving world as the "figure in the carpet" in James's fiction.

Springer, Mary Doyle. *Forms of the Modern Novella*. Chicago: University of Chicago Press, 1975. A penetrating study of the genre to which the late James assigned *Daisy Miller*.

Stafford, William T. *James's Daisy Miller: The Story, the Play, the Critics*. New York: Charles Scribner's Sons, 1963. A useful source book that includes the texts of *Daisy Miller* as story and as play, James's comments on the tale, and critical comments by contemporary and modern critics.

Strouse, Jean. *Alice James: A Life*. Boston: Houghton Mifflin, 1980. Prize-winning life of James's sister.

Tuttleton, James W. *The Novel of Manners in America*. Chapel Hill: University of North Carolina Press, 1972. An excellent study of the genre of *Daisy Miller*.

Vaid, Krishna Baldev. *Technique in the Tales of Henry James*. Cambridge, Mass.: Harvard University Press, 1964. An older, standard study of James's technique in his shorter fiction, which should be supplemented by reading of Cowdery, Kraft, and Springer.

Wagenknecht, Edward. *The Tales of Henry James*. New York: Frederick Ungar, 1984. Includes a lively discussion of *Daisy Miller* with long, informative footnotes about other commentaries on the tale.

Wasserstrom, William. *Heiress of All the Ages: Sex and Sentiment in the Genteel Tradition*. Minneapolis: University of Minnesota Press, 1959. Treats Daisy as not merely innocent but also as ignorant, childish, even infantile.

Wegelin, Christof. *The Image of Europe in Henry James*. Dallas, Texas: Southern Methodist University Press, 1958. James attacks "American snobbishness abroad" and decries the death of individual responsibility at the hands of convention.

West, Rebecca. *Henry James*. New York: Henry Holt & Co., 1916. One of the earliest book-length studies of James.

Yeazell, Ruth Bernard. *The Death and Letters of Alice James*. Berkeley: University of California Press, 1981. A long interpretive essay introduces Alice James's letters.

Articles and Parts of Books

Barnett, Louise K. "Jamesian Feminism: Women in *Daisy Miller.*" *Studies in Short Fiction* 16 (1979):281–87. James contrasts Daisy's desire for freedom with the confinement of other women to socially approved but sterile feminine existences.

Bosanquet, Theodora. "The Revised Version." *Little Review* 5 (August 1918):56–62.

Branch, Watson. "'The Deeper Psychology': James's Legacy from Hawthorne." *Arizona Quarterly* 40 (Spring 1984):67–74. Relates *Daisy Miller* to Hawthorne's "Rappaccini's Daughter."

Buitenhuis, Peter. "From *Daisy Miller* to *Julia Bride.*" *American Quarterly* 11 (Summer 1959):136–46. Daisy is a flat character compared to James's more critical and sophisticated characterization in "Julia Bride."

Coffin, Tristram P. "Daisy Miller: Western Hero." *Western Folklore* 17 (October 1958):273–75. James gives Daisy "the very personality traits that we have for some time now recognized as those of the western hero."

"Contributor's Club" [unsigned; Constance Fenimore Woolson]. *Atlantic*

Monthly 43 (February 1879):258–59. Daisy "an exquisitely loyal service to American girlhood."

"Contributor's Club" [unsigned: John Hay]. *Atlantic Monthly* 43 (March 1879):252–62. "All poor Daisy's crimes are purely conventional." James "loves her and admires her."

Davidson, Cathy N. "'Circumsexualocution' in Henry James's *Daisy Miller.*" *Arizona Quarterly* 32 (1976):353–66. The fear of sex and its repression comes out in the circumlocutions of the characters.

Deakin, Motley. "Daisy Miller, Tradition, and the European Heroine." *Comparative Literature Studies* 6 (March 1969):45–69. Suggested sources in Sand, Turgenev, De Staël, and Cherbuliez support a view of Daisy as a martyr to freedom.

———. "Two Studies of *Daisy Miller.*" *Henry James Review* 5 (Fall 1983):2–28. Perhaps the best recent essay; part 1, "*Daisy Miller* and Baedeker," discusses the use of setting and the meaning of the locales for nineteenth-century readers; part 2, "Poor Winterbourne, Poor Little Daisy," concentrates on point of view, style, and tone to interpret James's attitudes toward Daisy and Winterbourne.

Draper, R. P. "Death of a Hero? Winterbourne and Daisy Miller." *Studies in Short Fiction* 6 (1969):601–8. Winterbourne as an indecisive character, similar to T. S. Eliot's Prufrock.

Dunbar, Viola. "A Note on the Genesis of *Daisy Miller.*" *Philological Quarterly* 27 (April 1948):184–86. Sees Cherbuliez's *Paule Méré* as a source.

———. "The Revision of *Daisy Miller.*" *Modern Language Notes* 65 (May 1950):311–17. Expresses the minority viewpoint that the 1909 text of *Daisy* is superior to the original.

Editorial [unsigned]. *New York Times*, 4 June 1879, p. 4. Mentions the controversy in New York society aroused by *Daisy Miller.*

Eliot, T. S. "On Henry James." In *The Question of Henry James,* edited by F. W. Dupee, 108–19. New York: Henry Holt, 1945. Reprinted from the *Little Review* (August 1918); includes Eliot's remark that James's mind was so fine that "no idea could violate it."

Gargano, James W. "*Daisy Miller*: An Abortive Quest for Innocence." *South Atlantic Quarterly* 59 (Winter 1960):114–20. Winterbourne as central character, a Puritan flawed by a "fatal coldness of heart."

Gibson, W. M., and G. R. Petty. "Project *Occult*: The Ordered Computer Collation of Unprepared Literary Text." In *Art and Error: Modern Textual Editing,* edited by Ronald Gottesman and Scott Boyce Bennett, 279–300. Bloomington: Indiana University Press, 1970. The appendix lists variants between early and late versions of *Daisy Miller.*

Grant, William E. "*Daisy Miller*: A Study of a Study." *Studies in Short Fiction* 11 (1974):17–25. A Winterbourne-centered reading with interesting observations on the name symbolism in the tale.

Hocks, Richard A. "*Daisy Miller*, Backward into the Past: A Centennial Essay." *Henry James Review* 1 (Winter 1980):164–78. The author's reading with reference to the first hundred years of critical commentary.

Howells, William Dean. "Henry James, Jr." *Century Magazine* 25 (November 1882):25–29. The essay, which includes Howells's praise of *Daisy Miller*, was illustrated by a copy (signed by Henry James) of the Cole engraving used as a frontispiece for this book.

Hoxie, Elizabeth F. "Mrs. Grundy Adopts Daisy Miller." *New England Quarterly* 19 (December 1946):474–84. Discusses the use of Daisy as a negative example in late nineteenth- and early twentieth-century handbooks on manners and etiquette.

Kennedy, Ian. "Frederick Winterbourne: The Good Bad Boy in *Daisy Miller*." *Arizona Quarterly* 29 (1973):139–50. Winterbourne as central character and as a "potential sexual monster."

Meyers, Jeffrey. "Velázquez and 'Daisy Miller.'" *Studies in Short Fiction* 16 (1979):171–78. Develops thematic implications of James's use of the Velázquez portrait of Innocent X in *Daisy Miller*.

Monteiro, George. "'Girlhood on the American Plan'—a Contemporary Defense of *Daisy Miller*." *Books at Brown* 19 (May 1963):89–93. Assigns the March 1879 comments on *Daisy* in the *Atlantic* to John Hay, not to Howells.

———. "William Dean Howells: Two Mistaken Attributions." *Papers of the Bibliographical Society of America* 56 (1962):254–57. Shows that two "Contributor's Club" comments on *Daisy*, long attributed to Howells, were in fact written by Constance Fenimore Woolson and John Hay.

Newberry, Frederick. "A Note on the Horror in James's Revision of *Daisy Miller*." *Henry James Review* 3 (Spring 1982):229–32. Argues that in the revision James has Mrs. Costello call Daisy a "horror" so that the reader can infer that Winterbourne has misheard her, hearing *whore* instead.

Ohmann, Carol. "Daisy Miller: A Study in Changing Intentions." *American Literature* 36 (March 1964):1–11. Argues that James's intentions changed as he wrote *Daisy Miller*, that he began writing a comedy of manners but finished the tale as "a symbolic presentation of a metaphysical ideal."

Pound, Ezra. "Henry James." In *Instigations*, 106–67. New York: Boni & Liveright, 1920. Includes Pound's introduction to the Henry James number of the *Little Review* (August 1918).

Randall, John H. "The Genteel Reader and *Daisy Miller*." *American Quarterly* 17 (1965):568–81. Winterbourne as point-of-view character represents the perspective of the genteel readers of James's time.

"Recent Novels" [unsigned]. *Nation* 27 (19 December 1878):387. A typical early review.

DAISY MILLER

Review of *Daisy Miller* [unsigned]. *New York Times*, 10 November 1878, p. 10. An example of an early, favorable American review.

Stone, Edward. "A Further Note on *Daisy Miller* and Cherbuliez." *Philological Quarterly* 29 (April 1950):213–16. Extends the thematic implications of the source suggested by Dunbar.

Tintner, Adeline R. "Two Innocents in Rome: Daisy Miller and Innocent the Tenth." *Essays in Literature* 6 (1979):71–78. Ironies of juxtaposing truly innocent Daisy with the Velázquez portrait of Innocent X, whose physiognomy conveys anything but innocence.

Volpe, Edmund L. "The Reception of Daisy Miller." *Boston Public Library Quarterly* 10 (January 1958):55–59. Presents evidence to refute the legend that the early critics expressed outrage with James over his depiction of American women in *Daisy Miller.*

White, Richard Grant. "Recent Fiction." *North American Review* 128 (January 1879):96–110. A favorable early review by an important critic.

Wood, Carl. "Frederick Winterbourne, James's Prisoner of Chillon." *Studies in the Novel* 9 (1977):33–45. Argues that Byron's "Prisoner of Chillon" is an important source for *Daisy Miller* and a key to its interpretation.

Bibliographies

Edel, Leon, and Dan H. Laurence. *A Bibliography of Henry James.* 3d. ed., rev. London: Rupert Hart-Davis, 1982.

McColgan, Kristian Pruitt. *Henry James, 1917–1959: A Reference Guide.* Boston: G. K. Hall, 1979.

Ricks, Beatrice. *Henry James: A Bibliography of Secondary Works.* Metuchen, N.J.: Scarecrow Press, 1975.

Scura, Dorothy M. *Henry James, 1960–1974: A Reference Guide.* Boston: G. K. Hall, 1979.

For studies of Henry James and of *Daisy Miller* after 1974, see the annual volumes of the *MLA International Bibliography*, the Henry James chapter in the hardcover annual *American Literary Scholarship* (Durham, N.C.: Duke University Press), and the annual reviews of James studies in the *Henry James Review* (Baltimore: Johns Hopkins University Press, 1979–).

INDEX

Index

Linton, Eliza Lynn, 17, 61
Lippincott's Magazine, 10
Lowell, James Russell, 13

Maves, Carl, 47
McColgan, Kristian Pruitt, 22
Meyers, Jeffrey, 20
Modern Language Association International Bibliography, 22
Monteiro, George, 19
Murray's Handbook: Rome and Its Environs, 42

Nation, The, 15
Newberry, Frederick, 20
New York Edition, ix, 7, 18, 40, 65, 87–94
New York Times, The, 14–15
North American Review, The, 15

Ohi, Dee Hansen, 20
Ohmann, Carol, 20, 67, 91

Petty, G. R., 20

Randall, John H., 21
Roosevelt, Theodore, 51
Rousseau, Jean Jacques, 42–43, 44

Sand, George, 19
Scura, Dorothy M., 22
Shakespeare, William: *Hamlet*, 9, 17, 40, 68; *Romeo and Juliet*, 68

Shelley, Percy Bysshe, 42, 48
Springer, Mary Doyle, 21
Staël, Madame de, 19, 42
Stafford, William, 22
Stephen, Leslie, 2, 12
Stone, Edward, 19

Tell, William, 45
Temple, Mary ("Minnie"), 63–64
Tintner, Adeline R., 20
Tocqueville, Alexis de, 42
Tolstoy, Leo, 9
Turgenev, Ivan, 5, 19, 65
Tuttleton, James W., 96
Twain, Mark, 19

Velázquez, Diego Rodriguez Silva y, 19–20
Volpe, Edmond L., 13, 19

Wagenknecht, Edward, 60
Ward, Mrs. Humphrey, 7
West, Rebecca, 1–2
Wharton, Edith, 7, 72
White, Richard Grant, 15
Wister, Owen, 7
Wood, Carl, 19–20
Woolf, Virginia, 2, 5, 54, 55
Woolson, Constance Fenimore, 13

Yeats, William Butler, 50

Zola, Emile, 5

ABOUT THE AUTHOR

Daniel Mark Fogel is professor of English at Louisiana State University. He is the editor and founder of the *Henry James Review* and the founder of the Henry James Society. His books include *Henry James and the Structure of the Romantic Imagination* and *American Letters and the Historical Consciousness: Essays in Honor of Lewis P. Simpson* (co-edited with J. Gerald Kennedy). He has edited three novels of Henry James—*The Princess Casamassima, The Tragic Muse,* and *The Reverberator*—for the Library of America. He is the author of scholarly articles on, among others, A. R. Ammons, S. T. Coleridge, Henry James, James Joyce, and D. H. Lawrence.